A Little Holy Disorder

A Little Holy Disorder

Rev. Frederick Schroeder
with Rev. Craig Meyers

VANTAGE PRESS
New York

FIRST EDITION

Copyright © 2002 by Rev. Frederick Schroeder
with Rev. Craig Meyers

Published by Vantage Press, Inc.
516 West 34th Street, New York, New York 10001

Manufactured in the United States of America
ISBN: 0-533-13949-X

Library of Congress Catalog Card No.: 01-126522

0 9 8 7 6 5 4 3 2 1

I want to thank

Rev. Craig Meyers for writing his memories of our joint pioneering ventures in ecumenism.

Fr. Leo Piquet for giving me the opportunity to be a senior pastoral associate.

Claire Magna, my present housekeeper, whom I have known since 1971, for jostling my memory on my years as a priest and for helping with the editing. She has been after me to write up a history of my life as a priest for a long, long time.

Patricia Wright, an English school teacher, married to a school teacher, whom I ministered to through sickness and death, helped.

and

Fr. Tom Conley and Patty Wright for their editorial assistance, and frequent, "Father, would you like to rephrase that?"

Contents

Preface

Why another book on the priesthood? There are several reasons. For one, as I examine my eighty-year relationship with the Church, I have a positive view of my vocation. Despite the recent scandals, I know that most priests are good, solid, God-fearing people. But along with many of my fellow clergy, I do believe the Catholic Church at times today is out of touch with reality. As necessary as authority is, hierarchical authoritarianism, especially if it is extreme, will not save the Church. I think the shepherding of its flocks is much more important. And I have had three major interests in my life as a priest that, I feel, can point the way to a better shepherding.

Spiritual direction has been a key factor in helping me make decisions for my own life and in providing guidance for others. In tragic moments early in my life and throughout these eighty-plus years of journeying to wholeness, I have needed and fortunately found spiritual directors. Without them, I certainly would not be in touch with God, with other human beings, or with myself. Without spiritual direction I wouldn't have made it to the priesthood, much less have stayed in my vocation.

So this is certainly one reason for my writing. I know we all, religious and laity, need and the Church must increasingly learn how to provide spiritual direction. Shortly after Vatican II, another clergyman and I wrote a book, *The Potential for Spiritual Direction in the New Rite of Penance.* The book is now out in a new edition, *Spiritual Direction for the Average Catholic.* In the twenty years that have elapsed since the first publication, I have seen more and more the value and need for priests and laypeople to have some type of spiritual direction. There are many ways people are seeking it—through counseling, support groups, etc.—but that is not the same as baring one's soul to another trusted human being. Through such moments we come to accept ourselves. We are most afraid of that which is uncertain, which requires struggle, which leaves us aware of our own mortality and human inability to transcend life's ambiguity. It is in the dire moments of uncertainty that we most need someone to listen, someone to help us through the crises, someone to help us get back in touch with ourselves and with God. I feel this is a primary function of the clergy that is frequently overlooked and yet can be an essential part of the sacrament of reconciliation.

The sacrament of reconciliation is, of course, part of the liturgy. And liturgy from the very beginning of my priesthood has been one of my main concerns. That interest was awakened early on, in my first theology classes. I learned then that in 1925 Pius XI, in instituting the feast of Christ the King, spoke of his purpose. He said that the faithful learn more by the annual celebrations of the feasts of the Church than by edicts from the Holy See. Another early influence was the magazine *Orate Fratres,* put out by the liturgical press founded by St. John's Abby, Collegeville, Minnesota. The liturgy is one of the primary sources of the renewal of the whole Church. Thank God, throughout my life it has been one of my major concerns.

Finally, I have felt throughout my career that we clergy need to return to the simplicity of Christ's ways. Like Jesus we need to go up and down the hills and valleys reaching out to individuals. We need closer personal contact with our parishioners. Somehow or other through most of my life it seems like the greatest liturgies have left people unmoved if they have had no personal contact with the clergy. How often we hear, "Father, you just don't understand." I think one of the things we priests need to do is have greater contact with the people so we do understand. Through my door-to-door evangelization, one-on-one relationships with my congregations, efforts to make the liturgy meaningful to the whole congregation, and spiritual direction I believe I have made a difference.

I know through the years I have become a better and a happier person—someone who at the present writing would like to live to be a hundred and to continue just what I am doing now. I hope it will be a help to you if I share with you the pitfalls and benefits of my life as a priest and as a human being.

A Little Holy Disorder

1

Out of Chaos

My early life was nothing if not chaotic. No matter how I interpret that early life, one thing remains clear: the Church and its influence on my family and the society in which I lived created in me the fear, insecurity, and pain from which I have fled all my life. But it is the Church, however, that has been my healer, the visionary answer to all the problems it helped create in me. The Church has always been both my damnation and salvation. It is that from which I flee and that toward which I run in anticipation. After eighty years it remains the focal point of my spiritual quest.

The story of Fred Schroeder as I know it did not begin at birth. I suspect that no one's story does. Our first years remain unknown to us except through the adult eyes of those with whom they are shared. The beginning of conscious identity starts with the awareness of ourselves in relationship to events that are marked on memory.

My story begins not with birth but with death: the death of my father. I am the only one of my brother and sisters who really remembers our father. He and my mother had five children in seven years. The oldest of the five, I was almost seven and my youngest sister was just three months old when my father died and left my mother to raise us by herself. When my uncle brought her home from the hospital where she had been staying by my father's bedside, praying for his recovery, my oldest sister remembers her screaming hysterically to us, "Your daddy's dead. You're orphans!" For a short while his death was not real to me. We waked him in the home. To me he looked just like my dad, but his stomach wasn't going up and down as I remembered it just before they took him to the hospital. Not till the funeral was over did I understand he was really gone.

He was a wonderful father, no question of that. My own recollections are no doubt colored by what our mother has told us: stories of a man who was good and kind, wise and gentle. My own sense of bereavement, the almost inconsolable feeling of loss, is a probable indicator that the essence of her portrayal contained more than a germ of truth. We were, however, probably also told some pious things like "God wanted him in heaven," for it wasn't long after his death that I thought, *How do I get to be with my dad?* At that time, in the 1920s, most people weren't aware of their unconscious emotions, but, in looking back, I'm sure I was literally dying to be with my father, because it was only a few months after he was gone that I got sick and almost died of pneumonia.

Partly from what I was told, partly from memory, I visualize those days in the hospital. They said I would die if I didn't fight back against the fluid filling my lungs. Back then there were no miracle medicines to intervene. If the body could not fight off the infection, death was inevitable. One night in the hospital my lungs were so full they put a tube in to drain them, but virtually nothing came out as I lay passively back and allowed the disease to have its way.

The nurses couldn't do anything to make me fight

back. Finally the doctor asked my mother, "Isn't there somebody who can get to Fred?"

Mother said, "Maybe his grandfather. He's very fond of his grandfather."

My grandfather was up in years. I can still hear him as he cried by my bedside, mourning another coming loss in the family, saying over and over how useless and how old he was and how helpless he felt, unable to make a difference. Yet he held me, he talked to me; he told me how he loved me, and he somehow prompted me to lie on my side despite the pain and allow the diseased fluid to drain. It did—all night long—soaking the hospital gown and the bed sheets until the lungs were clear and the recovery process began. When my grandfather came to see me the very next morning, I was sitting up in bed waiting for him.

It was not only my grandfather who helped me at this time. My father had had a really good relationship with a priest whom I highly respected and loved, and so I welcomed his visits and was quite willing to have him anoint me at this time. He, like the others, feared I was dying. I'm sure he asked me if I had any bad things I wanted to tell him about (my first confession), and he let me make my first Holy Communion. So at six-and-half I received three sacraments of the Church, which surely helped my recovery.

The importance of this event in my life cannot be overestimated. At a time when I felt so hopeless and abandoned that I did not want to live, an old man doubting his own value virtually brought me back to life through nothing but love and compassion. He was my first spiritual director. Somehow that man and his power and the priest and his ministrations in that moment touched upon many of my questions that have to do with success and the meaning of Christian vocation. That choice of mine to live, however, threw me into a chaos with which I would have to deal the rest of my life.

The first part of the chaos was internal. While I obviously loved my father and shared the opinion of my mother that he was a truly good man, I was also so angry with him that I have not been able to shake the resentment to this day. I have never quite gotten over the sense that he abandoned me, the feeling that if he had tried harder, been wiser, consulted a doctor sooner (as my mother said she suggested and his own mother fought against), I would not have been left without his love, nor would I have been exposed to what would follow. As I have heard the story, when Dad began to feel ill my mother urged him to go to the family doctor, and he assured her he would. But each time on his way to the doctor, he stopped by to visit his mother. She told him that all doctors ever wanted to do was operate, and she persuaded him to go to a quack. By the time our family doctor got to the case, it was too late. My father's appendix had burst before they could operate. My father had been twenty-eight when he married, and it seems likely that Grandmother Schroeder, although she didn't realize it, was angry with my mother for taking away her son. In her desire to cling to her baby boy, she unwittingly gave him deadly advice. But by the same token, he took that advice.

Often in my life I have made comparisons between what happens in my family and in the Church family. Just as the image of a mother is held up highly, so is the image of Mother Church. It blinds us to their faults. Mother Church evokes feelings of nurture and love, a forgiving and sacrificial presence that will always be there to sustain the child whatever the circumstances. We tend

4

to view the love of a mother as the closest thing to godliness we can imagine, and we expect to be nurtured.

If ever there was a family in need of the love of Mother Church, it was the Schroeder family not long after the death of my father. My mother was responsible for the rearing of five small children with no outside support. There was no sustaining care from the Church. I am sure there were well-meaning individuals who showed practical love, but I have no sense of being loved or nurtured by the Church after I returned home from the hospital.

For a short time after my father's death, things had gone relatively well for our family. He had been a shrewd businessman, friends with the banker, the priests, the man on the corner. Fortunately, three months before he died he had taken out an insurance policy that was a godsend. Like many folks with a sudden inheritance, my mother got a better car to drive. And at last she had her chance to fix up our house at 235 W. Broadway, in Mishawaka, Indiana. It was a typical twenties frame bungalow: living room, dining room, kitchen, one bedroom, and small bath down; three bedrooms and half-bath up. Mother added a sunporch, which was not really an extravagance. She said my sister Virginia, who was ill, needed it. A cousin carpenter did the work. I'm sure, for a short time, there were other improvements to the house. But soon the money ran out and not too much later the Depression hit.

Our relatives promised to help and, although they undoubtedly meant it, the Depression hit them too. All of us were suddenly poor.

The Church also felt the pinch. As the Depression deepened, our local parish needed money. Soon each Sunday and Holy Day, ushers were at the door collecting twenty-five cents from each adult and ten cents from each child. From those dimes our family could make a meal, so we children sneaked into Mass without paying—a venial sin—to avoid the mortal sin of not attending Mass. In the inflexible rigidity of the Church, it was a mortal sin to miss Mass on Sunday. You could burn in hell forever!

Today, of course, the Church is more nurturing. Vatican II reminded us that the Church is the whole people of God. In a practical way we have always known that. In the past, however, the Church was seen as the hierarchy that interprets the truth and the priests who proclaim it. This is still true, of course. But now the Church is also seen as the structure that binds us together in service. The Church is the storekeeper down the street, the old woman up the block, the child in the classroom, the police officer on the beat. The Church is the people who mirror the attitudes and views of the overall body. But this was not our understanding in 1929.

Since neither our relatives nor the Church could help, we children who were old enough pitched in to help my mother provide. We fixed bunches of rhubarb and asparagus, selling them for ten cents apiece or three-for-a-quarter. It was a buy! Although I was hardly old enough, I got a paper route. Sometimes on a weekday night my mother would be hopeful I could collect twenty cents from someone who had not paid the bill for the paper on the previous Saturday. We could make a meal with twenty cents. It was my job to go to the store with that twenty cents to buy a nickel's worth of hamburger and a loaf of bread, a head of cabbage, or a few potatoes. It embarrassed me to shop like a pauper. I hated it. But that would spell supper for the six of us.

We children would take turns answering the door to tell bill collectors, "Nobody's home." Some bills had to be paid, however, or we ended up with no lights, no heat.

And although one of my sisters remembers going up to the railroad tracks to pick up coal that bounced off coal cars, we couldn't collect enough there to fill our bin.

I relish one incident. Desperate for cash, Mother and I gathered up a whole wagonful of toys, old Christmas presents, outgrown clothes—some good things—and went downtown to a secondhand store man. We asked him, "What can you give us for these treasures?"

He surveyed the lot carefully and finally said, "Can't give you a penny more than five dollars."

We both almost jumped out of our skins. A fond memory was our joyous affirmation of "Schroeder and Son, Junk Dealers." Afterward, our trips to the junk man became a regular practice.

It wasn't so bad that we were poor people and therefore lumped into a class that only Jesus could really love. What was more important was that a few years after my father's death we had become a family that was no longer respectable. Since my mother was still a very attractive woman, as time passed it wasn't surprising that a man or two paid her some attention. But any time she dated tongues would wag, and when she had the temerity to date a divorced man, the gossipmongers really had a field day. Then that man came to live with us. We children were called downstairs and told he was our "new daddy." We didn't want a new daddy. We wanted our old daddy back. And for a few years life for all of us was pure hell. Once when he physically threatened my mother, I came at him with a raised baseball bat to defend her. Because both my mother and the man were Catholics, good Catholics, believing in their hearts they were committing an unforgivable sin, it is possible that guilt brought on much of their angry quarreling. If the Church had allowed them to marry, perhaps we could have been a family. But that was not the case. And of course, the gossipmongers had the backing of the Church in their disapproval. We all were hurt. We children felt we were a scandal in the parish.

When, several years later, the man left and my maternal grandmother came to live with us, an element of stability was added to our physical living conditions, yet my feelings of being morally unworthy and socially unacceptable were not changed. The chaotic emotional status that had shaped my identity up until that time remained dominant. As a twelve-year-old boy who had no special talents, I yearned for any way out. And it was to the Church who had acted as my judge and accuser that I looked to for relief.

Why not become a priest? I thought. When I have been asked about my call in later years, I have searched for an appropriate answer. I have wanted to speak of the guiding hands of priests and sisters who recognized my talents at an early age. I have wanted to describe the origin of my vocation in terms that could stimulate others to become priests and do honor to the Church. I have wanted all those things, but they aren't there. I made the decision to enter seminary because, although I didn't know it at the time, I had nowhere else to go. And the Church received me with less than overwhelming enthusiasm. If destiny means the systematic elimination of all other choices, I think I was destined to become a priest.

It is not that I did not hold the Church in highest reverence. From the standpoint of my own tainted position and less-than-lofty self-esteem, I viewed the Church with awe. I thought the truly holy people, the wise and worthy, served in the Church. It was not out of lack of respect for the Church, it was out of lack of respect for myself that I hesitated to take the possibility of becoming a priest with any seriousness.

Nor was I without desire to have a vocation to the priesthood. I had been so moved by what my grandfather had accomplished in my illness through love and concern and by the equally loving ministrations of a priest that I wanted a life rooted in helping people. In my own plight, I wanted the love I had heard taught in the devotions and lessons in parochial school to be visited on people like myself, my mother, my brother and sisters. If some of the nuns who taught me seemed without pity, the Lord they taught exuded the love I so desperately needed. Whether from timidity borne of my circumstances or by nature, I have always had a streak of tenderness that reaches out to those in pain. In my secret dreams the idea of a priestly vocation was deliciously attractive. In the world I occupied in waking moments, the risk of pursuing it was terrifying.

First of all there were my peers. I was afraid if I told my classmates I wanted to be a priest, they would laugh at me. Moreover, by now the Depression was taking its toll and families were scraping together all their resources to survive. The once-honored thought of having a son become a priest had given way to the harsh reality of losing another partial breadwinner who could help hold the family together. So when a youngster decided to become a priest, it was well known that he probably couldn't do anything else, that the Church would accept almost any candidate, regardless of talent, intellect, or virtue. For a person deemed by circumstances "least likely" to succeed, the choice of a priestly vocation seemed to be at that time a verification that success in any other field was beyond the would-be cleric's capacity.

Still I had a great fear of rejection. Could I approach

a priest and risk being turned away, even though the least likely candidates were being accepted? Could I handle the ridicule of my peers or the rejection of someone holy enough to know my real worth? Finally, in desperation, I had to find out. There weren't any jobs for us children who could work to keep up the household, and my mother couldn't work with four youngsters at home. (Our sister Virginia had died that year.) In desperation, Mother had sent my brother to a home and my two sisters to boarding school with the Dominican nuns in Adrian, Michigan, for a couple of years. Why did I think my mother could support me any more than them? But how to go about becoming a priest? I determined that I could expect no real support from my pastor, so I first broached the subject to a priest at Notre Dame.

Reared in Mishawaka in the very shadow of the Golden Dome, at that time I had as much faith in the priests there as I had in their football team which was considerable. To my surprise the priest neither laughed nor rejected my query but told me I would have to clear the process with my own pastor.

So I had no choice. Finally I got up enough courage to talk to the pastor, who I thought would surely kick me out. I was wrong. He simply asked, "What kind of a priest do you want to be—a parish priest or a university professor?" I didn't feel I could ever be qualified to be a university professor, but I genuinely wanted to help people, to be a pastor of souls.

Just as I was beginning to feel good about my decisions, what I feared most happened. My pastor, a busy priest in a large parish, felt it necessary to ask the nuns at our school about my capabilities, something about which they had never seemed too enthusiastic. And so it was that the nun we had dubbed Sr. Mary "Battle-ax" welcomed me to religious life. She walked into the classroom, faced me at my desk, and said loudly enough for all my classmates to hear, "You will never make a priest." So much for my auspicious start as a candidate for the Lord's work. "Least likely" was still an apt title.

However, despite everything, the other nuns and the pastor must have decided I should get out of the "bad, bad environment" that they apparently thought I was in. I skipped the eighth grade not because of brilliance but because I couldn't afford to stay at home any longer. The pastor made arrangements for me to go to the preparatory school (the high school that prepared young men for the seminary) at St. Joseph's College, Rensselaer, Indiana.

2

Under Orders

Certainly in my heart, I was determined to become a priest to help people. But subconsciously, I probably saw the Church as a way out of chaos. I subconsciously wanted order. My father was dead and my siblings were scattered. Poverty was driving my family apart, and I had no vocational prospects. I had been labeled unworthy. I had no benefactor and, thus far, life had not been predictable or controllable. The Church was the most visible, orderly, structured, and predictable element in my life, even if its predictability was sometimes painful.

The fact is that the yearning for stability in the human heart, the desire for a home base of belonging, is so strong that order is often sought at the expense of other vital aspects of our identity. There are many people whose early lives have been so traumatized by events beyond their control that they can only survive in institutions. Prison psychologists speak of those who are emotionally institutionalized. Once they are released, they panic on the streets and ultimately find themselves back in prison by choice. Children in families of abuse will often fight to stay in the environments that are known rather than be subjected to the possibility of more humane surroundings that are unknown. There is a stubborn desire for order that will lead us into thoughtless choices that are potentially more devastating than that from which we flee.

And so, as I said, my choice at this time to become a priest was not as thoughtful as it was desperate. Subconsciously I probably wanted order. And St. Joseph's was very well organized, but my first months there were not happy ones.

A boy from my home neighborhood who had entered at the same time as I felt it his Christian duty to help my new peers weed out an unworthy classmate whose tainted past reflected on them. He wanted to make my new life as miserable as possible, in the hope that I would see the error of my ways and return home, or wherever it was that I might fit in. He formed a group who called themselves the Five Aces, a group of boys who were determined to get rid of this unworthy kid.

One of my other classmates, who has been a great friend through the years, said, "Fred, when they rough you up, why don't you just push 'em over the banister and let 'em fall down on their heads even if it kills one of 'em?" That was more violence than I had in mind. Even if I had such violence in my nature, I would have been afraid of the consequences if not from the authorities, at least from the remaining Four Aces.

Within the structure of St. Joseph's, however, despite the hardships, I always found what I seemed to need. A midyear retreat touched the hearts of my tormentors. Moved possibly by the cruelty of their behavior (or more likely by some priest's admonition), they apologized, and my life began to progress without their daily taunts and assaults. I found friends to study with and socialize with. I began to enjoy my preparatory years.

During those six years, the seeds of my current questions about the Church were sown and the basis of my discontent was established, but on the surface I saw little to complain about or question. Since sex was rarely, if ever, a classroom subject and since I had been brought up with the idea of the hierarchy ruling the Church and the place of women being either the home or the convent, I didn't realize these were issues that later would trouble me. The essence of the Gospel that has kept me in the Church was taught in the classroom and lived in the community. I believed then and still do that God's forgiveness and grace were involved in the transformation of my adolescent tormentors into friends. The incident of the Five Aces would not be earth-shaking to anyone except a young boy whose very existence is at stake in fitting into the only environment that offers him hope.

Despite the hypocrisy always found in human institutions, the teaching, if not always the teachers, remained that compelling image of a God of such love that no living creature is outside the domain of his acceptance. And with all its faults, St. Joe's represented an institution that would take a young man with no prospects and offer him a life. We always have to measure things against real alternatives. My alternative, realistically, might have been taking off to God knows where, never to be heard from again as was often the case during the Depression. The life the Church offered me was a gift of grace.

Because of the Depression, many orders, including the congregation of the Precious Blood Order who staffed St. Joe's, combined high school and college into a six-year course. Having skipped the eighth grade and never being a large person, I was always behind. My high school and college years, therefore, were not distinguished by great success or failure. I was a fairly good student, however, and after the first year formed a few friendships that have survived the years. One friend in particular, Tim, came from a relatively affluent family, and he taught me some of the social graces I lacked at the time. The inexperience in the sort of gatherings required on a college campus only reinforced my sense of ineptness, coming from my background. Tim taught me the rudiments of appropriate table behavior and how to make polite conversation. For his guidance I am eternally grateful.

There were other friends whose memories I have cherished throughout my life. Francis shared his friendship with me—and sometimes staked me to things I couldn't afford. Bob, who would become a lawyer, was a classmate who provided me the opportunity to share ideas in philosophy classes, a chance to grow. I learned from Bob, also, to carry impressive armloads of books out of study hall across the campus where our studiousness could be viewed from the windows of the Faculty Building. There were others friends and details that are of no particular interest except to an old priest who reminisces about them.

Physically smaller than the others, I nevertheless tried all sports. Our team won the pennant, but as a seventy-five-pound freshman football player I only managed to get in one play. I was also the water boy. During the basketball season, I sat on the bench most of the time. Academically, however, I progressed acceptably. The longer I stayed at St. Joe's, the more important structure was to me. Despite a few, mostly hidden impulses toward rebelliousness, I felt safe and at home in my role as a preseminarian.

Now and then, however, the rebelliousness wasn't completely hidden. During my last year at St. Joe's, one of the priests got another boy and me to run the Raleigh Smoking Club. It was the college recreation center, a place to play pool and Ping-Pong, to hang out—and to smoke. No one was aware of the risk of cancer or heart attack back then. The big bonus about managing the club was that my share for the whole year was a total of seventy-five dollars. That was big money in 1934–35 (the yearly cost of my tuition, room, and board was only about three-hundred dollars). It was more spending money than I had had throughout the six years.

The Raleigh Club taught me a few realities not available in the classroom. I thought I should smoke since most of the club members did. Cigarettes I didn't like. I never got over their choking me—my lungs were probably still affected by my early bout with pneumonia. But determined to be one of the guys, I tried a couple of Kaywoodie pipes that a friend loaned me and finally one of my buddies offered me a chew that made me sick. My early illness had its blessing—I learned I could not use tobacco to bond with my friends.

I shared with them, however, an enthusiasm for football. St. Joseph's College had a good team, and we loyally watched and cheered for them. But when it came to the big college games, I rebelled against most of the faculty and many of my classmates. The Precious Blood fathers who ran St. Joseph's had schools at Carthagena and at Berkesville, Ohio, before they had St. Joseph's College at Rensselaer. They were for any Ohio school. Born under Notre Dame's golden dome, I was loyal to the Irish and had a chance while I was managing the club to prove their superiority. In my senior year, while everyone else was watching our team play, I was in the Raleigh Club listening to the radio coverage of the Notre Dame–Ohio State game.

What a game that was for Notre Dame! It was one of the first last-minute drills that worked for them. They scored two touchdowns and a field goal during the last few minutes of the game. Of course, we later knew it was the Hail Marys of the nuns in front of the radio that brought the victory. But my teachers and friends were stunned that their beloved Ohio State lost.

My rebellions, like this loyalty to Notre Dame, even when triumphant were minor. All in all, the Church provided me with grace, hope, acceptance, and, above all, order. And yet, it was during those school years that I experienced and was taught other things against which I have struggled most as a priest. Though the Church at its best could be gracious, giving, and forgiving, it could also be narrow, judgmental, and exclusive. Because of my desire—no, my desperate need for order—I would suppress my awareness of things that were wrong until they would surprise, even shock me years later.

World War II America and its aftermath saw the Roman Catholic Church come of age. As a nation we have not dealt well with racial division, but religious separation posed little problem after the war for a nation on the move. In fact, most Americans now can hardly remember when there was a "Catholic neighborhood" in their community.

This means that now Catholics, exposed more and more to the values and beliefs of their non-Catholic neighbors, question things that their parents accepted without question. They openly defy authoritative directives that their elders only quietly ignored. The behavior of Catholics has more and more reflected the open-ended nature of American political and social life. While American Catholics remain, on the whole, respectful of religious authority, they no longer automatically accept the conclusions of that authority as personally binding. Even the most conservative elements in the Church acknowledge that Pa-

pal decrees on such issues as birth control are largely irrelevant to the majority of contemporary Catholics. The consequence of this change is that we have a Church largely governed by people educated and shaped in my generation or the one shortly following but whose younger generations have entirely different views. Since we believe that the Holy Spirit guides the Church to constructive adaptation, change is necessary if it is to grow more Christ-like. However, the education, formal as well as informal, to which I was exposed feared any kind of change.

In recent decades, most of the truly divisive issues in our American Church have revolved around sexuality and the role of women in the Church. Homosexuality has always been a problem to some degree in the Church. Other issues, such as sexual misconduct on the part of priests, reports of pedophilia, the movement to discuss a married priesthood, and celibacy, have made headlines and created divisions that have shaken the Church from the local to the national level. The increasing voice of women asking for places of responsibility that match the level of their sacrifice continues to trouble the Church. No formal sign of change, of course, is evident at this time although the treatment of religious women has affected the loyalty of women parishioners in many ways. These are issues that we deal with now.

The issue of homosexuality is a prime example of the Church's contradictory attitudes. Homosexuality among priests has never been the problem the Church's more vehement detractors have claimed, but it has always been a reality despite the Church's denials. It has sometimes tragically led to the abuse of adolescent males by priests. It has sometimes shaped diocesan politics and has made and ruined careers. However, the Church holds firm to its moral teaching about the sinfulness of homosexuality and leads families, out of obedience to the Church, often to disown homosexual members. While lay homosexuals are stigmatized, ordained homosexuals are protected and quietly moved when there is the appearance of trouble. During my preseminary years special friendships were very much feared and frowned on, but homosexuality was not discussed formally. My lack of knowledge on this subject did not prepare me to deal with the issue whenever it arose.

How ludicrous this was for someone being trained to exercise moral authority could be seen in my dramatic career at St. Joseph's. We were an all-boys school. As in Shakespeare's day, that meant that somebody had to be chosen to play the female roles. As the smallest youngster and one whose voice hadn't changed when I entered the school, I got all the choice female roles. No one ever told me why some of the boys made jokes that I did not understand. So naive was I that it never crossed my mind that there was any sexual innuendo. Much later, I was thirty-seven years old and in my third parish, a shepherd of souls, before a good Catholic physician explained homosexual behavior to me—I remember incredulously exclaiming, "They do what?"

In the area of sexuality, Church leaders often make decisions that have unfortunate consequences. For instance, most studies have shown that there is a correlation between their endorsement of female subservience within families and the incidence of physical abuse. Their elevated view of the male priest and the subordinate image of the religious female confirm this view constantly.

In my preseminary and seminary education the position of women was dramatically impressed on us, not as a theological reality, not as a biblical principle, but as a personal threat. One of my close prep-school friends was pursuing a secular career. However, it became apparent that our relationship could not continue because of his growing interest in the relatively tame girlie magazines he became engrossed in and because of his trips to town to explore what might be out there. As future priests, we were warned about women. Somewhere between the seemingly contradictory images of the temptress Eve and the pure Mother of Our Lord were women out there wanting to corrupt us. Women were generically no good, but if they would accept their appropriate role as objects of service to their male counterparts, they could be transformed into something precious to God. But for us, we needed to beware of the horde of ravenous women waiting just outside the walls of our cloistered campus to tempt and corrupt us.

This view resulted in three things. First of all, even with religiously minded adolescents, the attraction of the ravenous seductress far outweighs that of the image of somebody's mother. The lonely wrestling with our sexuality at night in our rooms was made more difficult by the image that we were ready prey for a world of beautiful women who couldn't wait to get their hands on us. We were told that if we put a Roman collar around a lamppost some woman would eventually be making love to it.

Second, we were given a false sense of our own attractiveness, which made us potentially willing participants in flirtations that sometimes led to unanticipated consequences. Men who remained in the priesthood often caused emotional suffering for the women they were involved with. Others who decided to marry left the priesthood. Witness the exodus of great numbers of former priests.

But most tragically, this view of women causes priests, who could do so much to strengthen families and promote values, to dismiss with unconscious contempt the real heroines of the Church. Some clergy lose sight of the creative and faithful, committed, and powerful women who fill the pews of our churches. These women either willingly, without considering an alternative, or resentfully, because there appears to be no alternative, give up their capacity to inject into our Church the kind of vigor and spirit that seems so often to be lacking. The majority of women, seeing even the most dedicated and holy women in the Church relegated to menial positions despite their qualifications, expect and ask no more for themselves, no matter what their gifts.

These were the negatives of my prep-school education, of which I was only dimly aware. I was about to graduate from St. Joseph's, glad, I think, that I was "under orders." The chaos of my external life was gone. Certainly in my heart I was determined to become a priest to help people. But subconsciously, I probably saw the Church as a way out of chaos. I subconsciously wanted order. My father was dead and my siblings were scattered. Poverty was driving my family apart, and I had no vocational prospects. I had been labeled unworthy. I had no benefactor and, thus far, life had not been predictable or controllable. The Church was the most visible, orderly, structured, and predictable element in my life, even if its predictability was sometimes painful.

I had a focus, in some ways a good focus, on the place where truth could be found. But I also was being led not toward liberating truth but to narrowing views of myself, my future, my nature, and maybe even the majesty of my God. It would be in later years that I recognized the limi-

21

tations that I never realized at that time had ill-equipped me for the chaos of a world within and the real world without, with which we all must contend.

3

Close Order Drill

In some sense, I think my becoming a priest was a miracle of God's Grace, because anytime after I got to be sixteen or seventeen if I could have gotten full-time employment, I would have quit school instantly to help support the family. At the time I was ready for the seminary, my mother felt obligated to let her mother and one of her sisters move in. The sister needed more lift power to take care of my aging grandmother, who had been living with her. This helped our family financially, but it still wasn't enough to support us. My siblings took any jobs they could, whether paper routes, baby-sitting, or you name it. During the summers, I worked painting houses—eight, nine, ten hours a day at fifty cents an hour. I was tickled to get that much, but, again, it certainly wasn't enough to support a family. So with seven other graduates from St. Joseph's preparatory school, I headed for St. Meinrad's to become a priest.

My being admitted to the seminary wasn't a question of my intelligence. The shortage of priests isn't just a present-day phenomenon. The Depression was on and anybody who wanted to be a priest was more than welcome. Our pastor in Mishawaka was disgruntled in those days because he felt that everybody he sent to the seminary quit. He often asked me, "Well, Fred, when are you going to quit?" He also used to inquire if I had enough underwear, which always puzzled me. Maybe it was his way of caring about my welfare. Another pastor across town now and then by way of encouragement gave me five dollars, which was a small fortune in those days. Maybe our pastor didn't have it to give.

The bishop of Fort Wayne had decided that eight from St. Joseph's would go to St. Meinrad's. Up until that time most of St. Joseph's graduates went to St. Gregory's in Ohio. But Ohio, Indiana—it didn't matter to us. Getting way down to that southern Indiana seminary was our first big problem. And to us it was enormous. None of us had traveled outside our immediate northern Indiana areas. Finally, a friend assured us that we could meet a charter bus at Indianapolis and it would take us to the seminary. What a relief!

While we worried about transportation, another friend I met at St. Meinrad's, a redhead like myself but a very shy man, had a much more serious concern. St. Joseph's College had seen to it that we had the necessary attire to attend a seminary. My friend, however, had not gone to St. Joe's and he was sure he was going to have to give up the priesthood altogether because he couldn't afford a cassock. If someone had not given him one, he might never have become a priest—and, incidentally, he is a very fine priest. What a shame that rules, regulations, the fear of not complying perfectly could cause a man so much trauma over getting ready to enter a seminary.

As we rode the bus down to St. Meinrad's, however, none of us seminarians-to-be had the slightest idea of the rules and regulations that were ahead of us. On the bus, my friends from St. Joe's drank beer and kidded me because I couldn't drink. (Alcohol made me sick—still does.)

Every time a beer truck passed us, they yelled, "Hey, Fred's getting drunker!"

When we got to St. Meinrad's, we couldn't believe the "town"—population 103. The general store, one surely built in the 1890s, had a weather-beaten sign on the roof—THE MODERN STORE. That and a filling station were the town center. Not far down the road, the cold gray brick seminary sat high up on a hill. As the bus wound around, we could see one little lightbulb attached to a pipe between the church and the seminary. It was an eerie, beautiful place, but bleak. I remember my reaction as if it were yesterday. I thought, *My God, am I supposed to spend the next six years of my life in this dreary place to become a priest?*

However, the next morning was more cheerful. It was a sunshiny day. We were rested and hungry, so even the little breakfast of "nonsense" they called it, (they didn't know what else to call it) tasted good. It was some sort of a breadlike cereal.

Most of the other students at St. Meinrad's had had six years of prep-seminary there and they were already subdued, passive, quiet, dutiful—all those good qualities that show you are more dead than alive. We were rambunctious. We would slip out at night after hours—some to smoke, some just to talk. One night one little short fellow whom we were not particularly fond of was trying to tell one of my Mishawaka friends about the rules and regulations. My friend grabbed him by the collar and said, "Listen, you little sawed-off GDSOB." I think he jumped five feet off the ground. He'd never heard those words before. So we really brought some college atmosphere and life into the place.

At midsemester, right after Christmas, when we had had our exams, the rector called every student in. He was a firm but very kind, fatherly man. In no uncertain terms, however, he told each one of us from St. Joseph's that we had entirely too much college spirit. It's a blessing there were eight of us. He probably didn't want and the seminary couldn't afford to expel all eight. But he let us know that we needed to be much, much more disciplined. Order, was what we needed—order.

Order can be a great thing. It certainly is for football teams and bands and their fans. Being Catholic in northern Indiana and attending football games at Notre Dame provides one with opportunities to lose himself in one of the most chauvinistic experiences available. Sitting in the packed stands at South Bend in the late fall, watching a well-drilled team, knowing, as it always seems to be, that a national title may be on the line with each particular game, a Catholic experiences something that is almost more spiritual than the Mass. All the real and mythologized persecution of immigrant ancestors, all the separation that society may have once visited on the Catholic newcomers in American cities, seems to be exorcised as the Fighting Irish eliminate the enemy. And at halftime, when the Leprechaun exhorts even Catholics of German extraction to a fighting frenzy, the mood is further elevated by the entrance of the Notre Dame marching band.

Even for a person who is neither sports fan nor music lover, a well-drilled college marching band is a sight to behold. The order of a hundred musicians moving to one beat, forming intricate figures on the field, is the result of hours and hours of repetitious training. Early-morning practice, late-evening rehearsal, both go together to produce the Saturday extravaganza. Close order drill—now that is the secret of a perfectly ordered unit and symbol of what we want in a perfectly ordered hierarchy.

While endless repetitions for the college band planning for a half-dozen Saturday shows a year produce the anticipated end result, the nature of college students, with so many other influences affecting them, remains the same. When the game is over, all the pubs and fraternity houses in South Bend are full of young folks who have not checked their individuality at the ticket gate. The influence of their friends, the ever-present hormones, the challenge of new courses they are encountering in the classroom, all exert their various pressures to shape an individual.

It is when all life becomes close order drill that order becomes counterproductive. Seminary training for the future priest is close order drill, but unlike the training for either the band or the football team, this drill excludes all balancing influences. The exclusion of outside influences, particularly any relationship to the half the world's population who are female, is one of the means of developing total focus on the task. The learning is not designed to create cognitive growth, only conformity and obedience. Truth does not become the object of scholarly pursuit but conformity to the doctrines that are taught by our spiritually endowed superiors.

On the one hand, seminary education is a graduate school process that involves the mastering of complex subjects: language, theology, history. On the other, it is set within a system modeled after the most regressive understandings of authoritarian child rearing. The paddle is replaced with the punishing word, the withholding of approval. The more advanced a student becomes and the more desperately he desires graduation and ordination, the more he fears he might be expelled for disobedience to the system. Failure is not academic. It is almost seen as a sentence to hell.

In a cloistered environment, the whole process of education is borne of order, carried out within a completely ordered structure, and designed to perpetuate order. Questions are not easily tolerated. My classmates challenged my audacity in asking questions that they felt implied I wasn't seeking information only but suggesting alternatives to what the professor was saying. For example, we were taught from the very beginning of our Catholic education that the greatest mystery, the idea of the Trinity, three persons in one God, could only be known by divine revelation. I had read some place that the pagan philosopher Plato had the idea of the three-in-one. Since he had no knowledge of the Judaic-Christian beliefs, I questioned whether it was not possible that the idea of the Trinity could be conceived by the light of pure reason. I was not trying to be insubordinate when I questioned but only to grow in my understanding of my Christian faith supported by reason.

It is into this close order drill that was not the exercise of an afternoon but the total surrender of every phase of life that I had entered when I stepped onto the campus of St. Meinrad's seminary in the fall of 1936.

After our session with the rector, we knew we had to shape up. Order was the command of our day. Yet our discipline wasn't as strict as that in other seminaries. It was nothing compared to that of the Jesuits at Mundelein, Illinois. Mundelein had luxury we didn't have—a swimming pool, golf course. When we had mutton, they had lobster. But, thank God, we had the Benedictines. They had a sense of humility and kindness instead of the terrible discipline at Mundelein despite its wealth.

We didn't escape unholy order, however. We had the vice rector as a professor in several classes, Introduction to Sacred Scripture for one, which was a farce in comparison with modern Scripture scholarship. We studied everything but the Bible itself. The vice rector was a complete contrast to the rector. We used to rationalize that because the vice rector worked awfully hard, his recreation was to step out of his room and nail any passing seminarian to scold him viciously about anything that came to his mind. Probably it was part and parcel of his interpretation of "Holy Obedience," close order drill.

Fortunately, the older seminarians told us not to pay any attention to him. "Don't let him interfere with your vocation," they'd say. But he did manage to drive some people out. Had the other seminarians not warned me about him, I might have been one of his victims. He confronted me several times. I'd be fuming inside, but I'd just smile. One day he got so mad with me just standing there and grinning, he grabbed hold of me and shook me. "I mean it!" he screamed.

He was the exception, however. Most of our professors were not tyrants, but all of them believed in strict discipline. We were to be humble and to be quiet. The rector used to tell us, "This attitude must carry on after you are ordained. You shouldn't speak out in a group of priests for at least ten years." That was a good example of the distorted idea of Holy Obedience that existed at that time. (Thank God it isn't that severe today.) After that first semester, we adjusted pretty well.

The biggest struggle for many of us was getting used to philosophy and theology classes in Latin. Oh my, what a ridiculous thing that was. We all knew we had to understand the Mass in Latin—but all philosophy? All theology? In spite of the fact that I failed Greek and was the smartest dumbbell in Latin, I must have had enough intelligence to get something out of the seminary professor's speaking Latin the whole time. I could read the texts quite well, so I had help for listening. I could ask the professor questions in sort of pig Latin style and understand him. But for some of my friends, language, any language other than English, was an almost insurmountable challenge.

I remember at one examination when four or five of us were sitting for orals, my friend who resisted Latin was cutting up in class.

The professor said, "*Tacite, Al, vel extra portes.*"

After class Al rushed to get Hannigan, our class genius.

"What did the professor say?"

"He said, 'Shut up or I'll throw you out the doors.'"

"Oh, I thought it was something like that," Al sighed and went back to apologize.

Al had a great memory. Once he recited "*Status Questione,*" which is a whole half-page or more in Latin, and the professor said, "*Optime dixisti,*" which means you have spoken well." Then he continued, "*Salumodo una question,*" and asked a very simple question about what Al had just said. Al hadn't the slightest idea. (Incidentally, he finally buckled down and conquered enough Latin to survive the classes.)

There is no doubt that good scholarship requires the facility in the languages of one's subject. Latin, biblical Greek, and Hebrew are all valuable to the interpreter of Scripture and the ones who would carry on the tradition of the Catholic faith. But to truly gain an understanding of a subject and to be able to discuss it, delve into it, own it, it must be attached to the images and symbols by which one defines reality in ordinary life. The use of Latin not as a tool to learn but as a hoop through which we had to jump was a debilitating aspect of our educational process. As Chaucer long ago pointed out in *The Canterbury*

Tales, the use of language as an indicator of the intellectual gulf between speaker and listener was the perfect model for some priests to use to protect themselves from the laity they led. As long as Latin was the language of the Church, many laity regarded it as a kind of magic that only priests knew. So the laity obeyed the Church's edicts not by virtue of competence and trust in them but by blind faith that only the priests had the secrets of the mystery of faith and only they could dispense wisdom about life.

Order finally began to really oppress me. During my year before ordination I often felt like a kind of prisoner. That deacon year the rector said to me, "What are we going to do with you, Schroeder?"

I said, "I don't know."

He told my mother, "He's got great potential, but *I* don't know." The rector was *so* afraid I wouldn't be obedient.

As a youngster who was grateful for the escape the Church had provided from family and social chaos, I had entered the seminary with no intention of creating disorder. I was no rebel. But occasionally, I couldn't resist asking the heretical "Why?"

During all my years at St. Meinrad's, most of the time I was concerned with the task of keeping up with my studies. It was late at night within my own mind that other struggles became frustrating. It was then that I wrestled with issues that were shaping my moral identity.

I had been relatively well prepared for the rigors of academia. Although I was never an outstanding student, in most of my courses I could hold my own. Even now, however, I am amazed at how ill-prepared I was to encounter the larger questions of my own existence, much less those that had to do with teaching others about life.

My fellow students had often opted for the priestly vocation after an ordinary life in high school and even college that had included experiments in all the things I had stayed away from: girls, a normal social life—the things that most adolescents in our society seek out and couldn't avoid if they wanted to. My fellow students' worldliness confounded me, for I took with absolute seriousness such things as personal piety and moral purity. I was shocked and didn't really understand the quite unpriestly talk of my peers as they reminisced about forbidden subjects even as they studied for exams on theology.

Once when I went home, some of my cousins and former school friends wanted me to join them in a game of Spin the Bottle. When I was closeted with the girl my spin won me, I just stood there. Finally, she said, "Well, let's get this over with," and gave me a quick peck. It had never occurred to me that I was supposed to do such a sinful thing as kiss a girl. I guess I felt that while studying for the priesthood I shouldn't even look at a girl, much less kiss her. Remember, this was the 1930s.

It was this personal struggle with my sense of unworthiness for the priesthood that stands out in my seminary experience far more than any specific field of study. I could not set aside thoughts of a sexual nature, and to me, even the thoughts were indicators of my personal weakness. I was so unschooled in areas of a sexual nature that I am sure even my fantasies were so naive that they would seem ludicrous to my more experienced friends. Yet the inaccuracy of my night images did nothing to lessen their impact. Fear, self-doubt, and agonizing bouts with my vocational worthiness filled my seminary years, and I must admit that they have never fully been eliminated from my thought throughout the years.

It is at this point that I became aware, painfully

aware, of how little attention is given to the moral development and the spiritual direction of priests. When I approached a professor, or anyone in authority for that matter, with my doubts, I would be met with priggish scolding or an embarrassed avoidance. Now, much later, I know that the issues of morality were difficult ones because many of those in authority were wrestling unsuccessfully with the temptations of a sexual nature in their own lives. Still others were embarrassed to talk about a subject they were as ill informed about as I was. And then there were and still are those unfortunately, who see the priesthood as a vocation in which adherents should, by the nature of ordination, be automatically removed from the issues of real life. Either way, my seminary years, which could have been a time of growth and development, became a period of fearful repression and guilty self-doubt that did little to make me a self-confident advocate for the Gospel.

Fortunately, however, I was one of the lucky few who found someone to help me through my quagmire. It isn't enough to go to confession and accept the penance of saying three "Hail Marys." I needed a spiritual director, someone to listen. In my deacon year, I found that someone, the first of several who would provide me spiritual direction throughout my life. Fr. Damasus Winzen saved my priesthood. He was my spiritual confidant for about twenty years, until he died. Because he was a survivor of the horrors of World War I that had so devastated him that he required years of spiritual rebuilding through both psychotherapy and the nurture of the Church when it could be found, Father Damasus had become a spiritual director of sensitivity and skill. It was under his guidance that I began to look inside myself in ways that promoted growth instead of guilt. After hearing his sensible talk on the place of the Virgin Mary in the whole mystery of redemption (a concept I had wrestled with), I told him, "Now I can be ordained." To this day, however, I am sure that the greatest gift he gave me was not specific bits of wisdom but the knowledge that spiritual help was out there to discover if one kept looking.

But in the seminary environment, such help most often did not exist. The confessional was surely one place where one could expect to find spiritual direction. However, as I later realized was true throughout the Catholic world, often the priests did not use the confessional to help but to punish. And I still believe that one of the weakest links in the development of a more humane and effective priesthood is that their "education" does not supply stimulus and nurture for growth at the time that the seeking mind is most open to new insights.

Toward the end of my prep-school years I began to have vague questions about the nature of the Church, as it was, and nebulous hopes for what it could possibly become. I know, at least subconsciously, I questioned some of the elements of priestly preparation. And now as I look back, it does amaze me how each step in that preparation contains elements of a progressive initiation into a college fraternity or even into the military. The more unworthy an initiate and the more eager to belong, the more he has invested in ultimate success. This provides power for those who hold the keys to acceptance and exclusion and ritualizes all the steps to full membership. It is then natural that when the applicants become full members, exercising all the powers and privileges of their new status, they will act the same way as their mentors in exercising control. Victims of the most brutal fraternal hazing and victims of abuse in military boot camp all reveal the same motivation to be close members of their group. When they get past the novitiate stage, they are able to stand before new recruits and tell them, "If I had to do it, so must you." If not excusable, it is at least understandable that parish priests often become arrogant and self-centered, since the training always holds up those who have completed the course as heroes of the faith to be admired and held in awe. The payback for the new priest, once ordination is achieved, is the ascension to that exalted status.

The value of my reflections on seminary has to do with three characteristics I found there, which help shape and maintain some of the less flattering elements in the order of the Church's structure. Those three things that left the most lasting impression on me were the attitude of the superiors, the curriculum, which didn't relate to the real life in which we would be guiding people once in the parish, and the pervasiveness of sexuality as an experience that was never seriously discussed.

Now what do I mean by *attitude*? I certainly do not mean the particular characteristics of mean-spiritedness that seemed to mark some professors and priests at the seminary. The hurt I felt then has long since been outgrown as those personal experiences have given way to a sense of painful concern for the whole Church—meaning the people of God, *not the institutional structure.* Nor do I mean the immaturity of my classmates and myself as we reacted, first fearfully and then in infantile rebellion, to the rules and regulations and the petty administration of discipline.

By *attitude,* I mean the collective authoritarianism that seemed to hang over the whole institution like a pall of darkness. The Church saw itself as an orderly entity with each rule, each regulation, more important than people. My consciousness of this attitude of the Church has bothered me all my life. Thank God, since Vatican II the emphasis now is (or is supposed to be) on the whole people of God.

The purpose of seminary education was not to create in each priest the fullest intellectual and spiritual gifts to make the Church great but rather to create priests so uniformly obedient that the Church order as it then existed would not have to protect itself from any departure from that Church order. Spiritual questions, if of any personal depth, were treated as assaults on orthodoxy. I made the error on several occasions of revealing my doubts to those who instructed me in my development, academically and spiritually. I was told in each session with my campus spiritual director that real believers did not have such doubts and any serious questioning of faith issues would earn me a quick trip home, a home I long since had lost contact with, at least as a foundation for my future. I was terrified after each session with the man. (They didn't know what else to do with this particular priest, so they made him spiritual director; not much value was put on spiritual direction at this time, and this priest certainly wasn't any Fr. Damasus Winzen.)

I had some serious doubts about the validity of the Catholic Church in relation to its overemphasis on money, its lack of enough concern for people. Instead of helping me face my doubts and deal with them, this "spiritual director" routinely told me that with my attitude I couldn't possibly succeed. (In retrospect I have to laugh, "Ha, ha, I'm past eighty now and I think I have succeeded.") My director often asked me why I didn't just quit and leave. My sense of personal unworthiness that sometimes bordered on hopelessness was eventually relieved when my classmates and I confessed to one another that our "spiritual director" had urged *all* of us to quit and implied that *all* of us were unworthy.

The collective attitude of the seminary was, in a nutshell, that excellence was deviance, honest questions were proto-heresies, and education that taught a thirst for knowledge was a threat. The curricula in seminary reflected the attitude that governed the seminary.

Presumably philosophy is the search for truth and theology the search for God. All the great philosophers and theologians broke new ground in going beyond the understandings of their day in order to arrive at some new possibility. What marked a philosopher or a theologian was the very fact that he or she refused to assume that the traditions of the past represented all that could be known about creation and its creator. The disciplines imply that what was known is only a prelude to what can be known and the conclusions of any given day are the raw materials of each new generation's continuing pursuit of knowledge. We, however, were not taught how to think or even that thinking was a positive value. We were taught what others had thought, and the tendency to stray from established truth was viewed with more than a little displeasure.

The second most obvious fact about our curriculum was what was missing. Any serious attempt to provide studies that could lead to self-understanding or an understanding of the relational, social, or political and economic life of the folks we would help make decisions about those very things was scrupulously omitted. On our own we had study groups on sociology, labor, etc., which were not part of the curricula. Genuine use of the secular tools readily available, sociology and psychology, was suspect at best and demonized at worst. Our task was to tell people what to do, what God wanted them to do. In the harsh realities of everyday life, we offered no tools that would enable folks to do those things. The pastoral duties were very unlike the teaching by example, by common symbol, by parable and humor we see in our Lord. The pastoral duties were seen as passing on the rigidity of our learning process to those who would soon be under our authority.

The blind trust the priests were encouraged to embrace in seminary was the expected basis of successfully engendering obedience among parishioners. And Catholics were naturally obedient up until the sixties. The laity today has changed and grown more dubious about all the rules and regulations of their Church. Many of the priests have not changed, and the low morale among the clergy can be partially traced to the fact that they have been trained for a role that is impossible to fulfill successfully unless blind trust exists, a condition that has long since passed away in most parishes, particularly among the young members of the Church.

Finally, seminary experiences, and what I believe are the churchwide results of those experiences, would not be fully dealt with unless the whole issue of sexuality was discussed in some measure. In the seminary what little mention was made of boy–girl relationships was to warn us to view women as evil seductresses who need to be punished for what we wish we could do to them. It is for this reason, I believe, that the Catholic Church has not been in the forefront of advocacy on the part of spousal abuse, child sexual abuse, and the elevation of women to a position of true honor in home or society, much less the Church.

Because the whole issue of sexuality was not discussed in seminary, this is at least a significant part of the problem a priest has in providing leadership in the moral development of the young and leading in the training of people for successful marriages. He is the person who should be foremost in setting the moral tone of the community in which he works. He deals with sexuality in every phase of his ministry. Yet from his seminary experience he is woefully unprepared to understand the dynamics of a subject about which he is either piously glad to be ignorant or totally embarrassed. That embarrassment is transmitted in the brief mention in premarital instruction of things that the priest feels he has little business even thinking about.

I don't think I am different from most priests in my day, particularly those who committed to the priesthood relatively early in life. On a vocational track before we were fully aware of what was happening in our adolescent bodies, we only had vague memories of what we heard or saw when boys and girls got together. We had had little or no personal experience. I remember going home to Mishawaka one summer only to experience the kiss of a young woman. I know she would have explained it to her parents or anybody who might ask as a sisterly show of affection, but it didn't affect me that way. So strong was my arousal at that single encounter that I doubted my vocation and considered leaving the seminary. In one of the few honest encounters with my campus spiritual director during that time, I was told, after an anguishing confession of my carnal weakness, not to dump all the hard work and commitment I had invested in seminary because of one minor transgression. He recommended I see Fr. Damasus Winzen because he had great insight into the human soul. I was glad I took the advice. That was the first occasion I had to seek help from Father Winzen. Still, the intensity with which that one seemingly insignificant event controlled my whole frame of reference for a relatively long time is an indicator of the extreme pressure of living celibate lives, with only a celibate future to anticipate and the hormones of a normal young person working their way without any volition on my part.

Homosexuality, if we are to believe sociological studies, is a condition that involves anywhere from 5 to 10 percent of the population. It is natural to assume that homosexuality exists at a higher rate, at least behaviorally, when the option of heterosexual relationships is denied, as in prison populations, all-boy schools, the military up until recently, and the priesthood. But this, too, was an issue that was not specifically addressed in the seminary.

I am not all that attractive and have little to offer that would make me an especially attractive target for anyone, male or female. However, in seminary I was overtly approached for homosexual intimacy twice. (I am sure, due to my naïveté, I was perhaps approached more often subtly but just didn't have a clue as to what was going on.) In the first instance, a classmate with whom I had struck up a friendship wanted to engage in kissing that was not fraternal. Even a person as backward as I was knew what was happening. It was the nature of our community that since the attempt was not aggressive or persistent, we remained friends with the clear understanding of the limits of our relationship. The second instance was different. A peer with whom I had shared deep emotional feelings, with whom I had shared my emerging philosophical ideas about the meaning of life and all those things students take so seriously, accompanied me on a walk in the woods. What he showed me was unmistakably an intention of seduction. Alone, feeling insecure, I reacted with the sort of homophobic panic that is instilled in us all—I beat the living daylights out of him. I am not a fighter, but neither was I a lover, at least in that context. I suppose what is significant for me in these encounters is that while the Church officially held up homosexual behavior as sin, unless the behavior was overtly disruptive, with the full Church's full knowledge these folks were passed on to their eventual priestly functions, and neither they nor their colleagues nor the parishioners were given any tools to deal with what could be extremely destructive. In the best-case scenario, priests who do not know anything about sexuality remain feeling frustrated, lonely, and always just a little bit guilty. The worst-case scenarios are seen in the ever more frequent stories of people who do not know the difference between sexual identities and tendencies and active predatory behavior.

I am convinced that the Church and all its priests need to attend more to the difficult but essential task of encouraging seminarians to think, to understand as much as can be taught about themselves and those they will be expected to guide. They need to be encouraged to exercise their creative potential, to fill themselves with dreams of coming up with innovative ideas and new concepts and truths every bit as important as those they read about. This might mean trusting that vocational commitment is born of genuine spiritual belief and integrity instead of being created by fear, punishment, and an invitation to return to the womb.

4

Testing the Limits

Some of us are slow learners. Maybe others of us are simply learning while we are doing and fail to realize what we have learned until some crisis or issue emerges. Given my oft-admitted naïveté and my genuine desire to serve in ways that help people and, I believe, given an honest absence of any real ego needs in terms of career goals, it is not surprising that it took me nineteen years after seminary to shape the ministry that I consciously have pursued in the latter part of my career.

I spent three years in Elwood, Indiana, and then three more years in Kokomo. That was followed by six years in Monterey and then seven in Union City. I learned in all those instances while I served as faithfully in my pastoral duties as I could.

In Elwood, I tried on my ministerial shoes, elated by ordination, eager to be about the work of the Lord. I learned in Kokomo to give up my fear of superiors. Lack of blind respect for leaders after viewing the professional life of one of them led me to the sense to judge people, even myself, on character and competence. Here I was allowed to do the kinds of things that later would become a part of my ecclesiastical value system. At Monterey and Union City, I was a part of creating the Church of the future. In my first parishes, I learned much about all those things they wouldn't think of teaching in seminary, those things that taught me to be a priest.

In my first two assignments, I had two different experiences as an associate, the first reinforcing everything I have come to believe about the structure at its worst, the second allowing me to know that even in a closed system, people can choose to let light in.

If indeed the primary purpose of recruitment, early religious experience, and training is to produce functionaries for the system, dependent in the early years and committed to the only system they know in later years, then Elwood, Indiana, continued the process with a vengeance. Dependency! Let me give an example.

Coming out of St. Meinrad's newly ordained, I was sent home for a brief visit and then to Elwood. It has surprised me ever since ordination how many large, beautiful churches there are in relatively small communities. Even today St. Joseph's Catholic Church in Elwood has only 396 families. When they built the church in 1889, however, the founding fathers thought the town would grow and be forever prosperous because it had natural gas. They thought the supply was unlimited and used it to light the streets at night and of course supply the churches. By the time I arrived in 1942, the handsome brick church had a two-story rectory beside it that had been built for two priests and a housekeeper. I had a regular suite of rooms: a sitting room, bedroom, and bath. Downstairs were the living room, dining room, kitchen, and offices. However, despite the elegance of the church and rectory, Elwood was not a happy assignment for me.

The general rule was that a new priest could not have an automobile until at least five years in the ministry. As a new priest I had few social skills and no vocational possibilities outside the Church. After all, how many employers are looking for someone whose primary skills are saying Mass in Latin and isolating himself from the community in terms of normal social intercourse? No ties, no transportation, no recourse, the neophyte is sent to a strange town under the complete authority of a priest whose primary concern often is making sure that the associate is no threat to his image and that the world and the associate understand the huge gap between the pastor's august role and the menial nature of his errand boy's function. By the time this not exclusive but very typical pattern was processed, the developing priest was a twenty-five-year-old adolescent with no inner strength, no self-confidence, and an unhealthy dependence on a system all too willing to do his thinking for him. In the 1940s this was the process. It has become more sophisticated in succeeding decades, but the basic components and motivations of the process are all too often visible even today.

The pastor at Elwood was a relative newcomer, only having been in that parish for a year or so. His primary task seemed to be in making sure that the memory of the previous associate pastor was totally discredited. That associate I soon learned had served with skill and faithfulness for some time, developing a strong popular following in the process. Any good thing said about him, however, the new pastor saw as an attack on himself, his own competence. It was soon clear to me that the second task of this pastor was to make certain that his new associate never achieved any status that would challenge the pastor's position.

Shortly after arrival in the early summer, I was told that there was little to do during that season. I helped with weekend Masses but was sent home during the week. It was obvious the pastor did not want me around.

With no other means of transportation, I took a train from Elwood to Logansport, a bus from Logansport to South Bend, and then someone from my home in Mishawaka had to pick me up. That went on for the whole summer. When I arrived home week after week my family and relatives wondered why I, just ordained, would be home on vacation. I imagine the people in the parish were told that I was lazy and had no vocational commitment or initiative.

When I was in Elwood, the pastor moved me about from job to job. Each time I appeared to be succeeding in a position, he shifted me to another, where I am sure he hoped I would fall on my face. Every year I was given a different program to direct. The first year, I taught religion to all eight grades and two years of high school. My seminary years hadn't prepared me to be an elementary or high school teacher. I was trained to be a priest. Evidently, however, I succeeded in relating to the youngsters, because the second year the pastor moved me out of the schools. I was put in charge of CYO (Catholic Youth Organization). The third year, he said, "We are neglecting the young ladies' sodality." Catholic Action was the in thing at the time, so he suggested, "Why don't you form some groups for the young women on Catholic Action." That was quite a chore. But here, as in all other tasks I was given to do, as soon as I got something going, the job was given to another and a new area was put under my charge. I was set up to fail and in those instances where sheer persistence bred success I was made to feel like an insubordinate subordinate but, above all, a subordinate.

I wrote about my concerns to Fr. Damasus Winzen, the Benedictine who had been so helpful to me as a spiritual director during my seminary years. Mercifully, he, who was to be my spiritual director for the next eighteen years, took me under his wing. Through him and through Fr. Michael A. Mathis, of Notre Dame, I developed ideas and attitudes that were productive in my priesthood. During the second summer at Elwood because the pastor was still delighted to have me out of his sight, I spent several weeks at Notre Dame working with Father Mathis on finding the real meat and meaning of the liturgical text both in the Breviary and in the Mass. And later that season, Father Winzen had me stay with him at his priory in Keyport, New Jersey. My self-esteem, which in Elwood was so low, was well bolstered. Father Winzen had me help him write a series of sermons for one of the dioceses in the East. Granted, I mostly typed what he said, but what a great privilege it was to work so closely and intimately with two great forerunners in the liturgical movement in the United States.

When I was with Father Winzen, once a week our reward was to go to New York City and take in a stage play. My first touch with the theater, it was a very broadening experience. I'll never forget the great play *Life with Father*. The opening scene was with the terrible-tempered father reading the newspaper. He saw something he didn't like, stomped his foot on the stage floor, and uttered a very loud, *"damn!"* The maid jumped two feet. Father Winzen liked that approach. He had lectured all over the world and had a great (and loud) speaking voice. The priory had a new maid, and every once in a while when things weren't going right, he would stomp his foot on the ground and utter a, *"damn"* that reverberated through the walls. What still amuses me to this day was the sound of that word echoing through the monastic walls. Of course, at the time we were the only ones in the monastery. Father Damasus was too kind to really scare a little maid.

Thinking back to my New York theater experiences that summer, I remember one play on Broadway I was sure was one I would not be allowed to see—*Ca-ROUSAL.* (I'd never heard the word *carousel.*) Naturally, we weren't alone in the monastery all the time, and a monk who taught drama assured all of us that the best thing on Broadway was *Carousel.* I was shocked. I was sure that there was no way I would be allowed to see—*Ca-ROUSAL.* Then there was another I was sure was taboo (even though Carol Burnett was one of my favorite stars)—*Once Upon a Mattress.* During these formative years, my whole perspective on life was wonderfully broadened because my pastor at Elwood couldn't stand the sight of me or any other insubordinate.

Those summers I spent away from Elwood led me to begin to understand the weaknesses, more accurately the perversions, of the Church, to which I had committed my entire life. I began to see that a vocational existence could be based on sham. If I wasn't careful, my goal could end up being not to serve Christ but to survive the early years so I could climb the ladder of success in a structure that would make me just like those I was growing to despise. That put incredible pressure on the conscience and emotions of a young man who thought, in all sincerity, that he was a devoted instrument of God's work.

While the summers were very rich, the winters were long and cold. Many nights I struggled with the loneliness, and often those long winters I would go alone into the sanctuary, hug the tabernacle, ask God for guidance. I don't believe that it is heresy to suggest that had this struggle gone on and on, had there been no spiritual guidance from Father Damasus, I might have become a bitter, frustrated priest who when my day came would be just like the pastors I disdained.

47

In 1945 the two dioceses of northern Indiana were divided into five and we had a new bishop. As the new bishop was preparing parish assignments, he asked his chancellor, who knew the diocese, "How long has Fred been with that pastor in Elwood?"

When he heard, "Three years," his immediate response was, "Good Lord, we've got to get him out of there." And so he sent me to Kokomo.

My new pastor, Father Bob Halpin, because of a speech impediment was no great preacher, but he was one of the brightest and most humble men in the diocese. He was a monsignor, but he insisted on being called Father because he maintained that was the only decent title for a priest. He was simply a good person, a hard worker, and a competent priest who never let ego get in the way of serving his people and helping his subordinates develop. I admired him very much. He was one of the best blessings of my life.

It was in that setting that I began to see the power of the Mass for a people who believed greatly in its practical efficacy. Yet because of my work on the liturgy at home in private and during those summers at Notre Dame, I began to question how words that people could not understand could actually help them grow. The pastor, however, was not ready to even think about changes in the liturgy, although he was willing to listen to my "dreams." He was, however, ready and more than willing to allow me, for the first time, to take on pastoral responsibility and make decisions. He asked me, "How could you be a priest for three years and not ever have anointed anybody?" I explained that my previous pastor had never allowed me to so.

I remember the first time I was called to a dying man's side to anoint him in what we then called the final or extreme unction. I was fearful and hesitant. I knew the words, but I wanted to be a genuine presence. I worked with the gentleman, dying with cancer, in those following weeks until he died. Moreover, I did for him a funeral Mass that had meaning precisely because of the relationship I had with him.

During those hours at his bedside, we had discussed the issue of his former life in relationship to his terrible illness. For the first time he dealt with the grace of a God who was not punishing him but suffered with him. And all this time, his first wife, who, after three successors, had returned to care for him, watched in silence whenever I came. She wasn't Catholic. One day when I was trying to comfort her husband, who persisted in believing that his current suffering was a result of his previous sins, I told him that we had just buried a wonderful lady who I don't think had done any serious wrong during her whole life, yet she suffered a brutal illness, an agonizing death—certainly not punishment for her sinning. Suddenly from the kitchen came his wife's remark, "Humph, there must have been a leak someplace." When I went to question her remark, she frowned. "Nobody's that perfect," she said. We had several talks after that, but I didn't feel my words had any effect on her.

After his death, however, I decided to look the lady up and, when I found her, was surprised at her warm greeting. She said, "I was just thinking about you. When does that convert class start?" At my invitation she joined the class, and she turned out to be an inspiration to us all.

Our church was a long way from her home, and we all marveled how she would walk across town in the worst winter weather to be present at this class. Once in a while she would come up with a piercing question, piercingly loud. For example, about the Trinity, she called out, "How can that possibly be?" Whenever that happened, I would walk over to where she was sitting and explain it to her and the whole class would drink in every word of explanation of a doctrine they had hesitated to question. From a totally unlearned but life-taught sincerity she was a breath of honesty for the whole group.

Because of her honesty she enabled the group to be more forthright about their convictions or prejudices. For example, a nurse from a Jewish hospital asked me if she, in order to become a Catholic, had to believe that a black person had a soul. One of the local residents from Kokomo, where we had a sizable black population, responded with a wonderful defense of black people. But when he finished he asked, "How could you put up with those Jews in that Jewish hospital?" And she then gave a magnificent defense of the Jewish people.

I stood back and laughed, saying, "Don't you see this is a perfect example of how easily we succumb to prejudice?" In this and many similar experiences, I was allowed to learn to be a pastor of souls. It was here that I began to personalize the amazing relationship in the Gospel between sincere service and self-giving evangelization. When the presence of Christ is in the priestly function, the response of the people does not have to be manipulated, cajoled, or pursued with anger, bigotry or gimmickry.

My pastor was a man of integrity within the community of priests, existing in a town that was neither very Catholic nor very Christian. Kokomo was still in the 1940s a center of Ku Klux Klan activity. I remember having to ask our housekeeper to fix supper for myself and a visiting black priest because I knew he would be refused service if we went to town to eat. While no activist by later standards, my pastor stood for the best that the Church proclaimed. We would travel together, and in a way that was never patronizing he taught me what he had learned. He made me feel part of a priestly team rather than a subordinate. He was happy to share with me the priestly functions such as presiding at baptisms, funerals, and Christmas and Holy Week Services. His example of generosity taught me the importance of sharing with my own associates when I became a pastor.

Father Bob was much respected in all the Catholic organizations in Kokomo and very active. But on one occasion I attended a Knights of Columbus meeting without him because he was elderly and not feeling well. The pastor of the other parish in town together with the hospital chaplain suggested that the K of C start having an open bar. I knew Father Bob felt drinking was a real problem and would have been much against their serving liquor. When I voiced my concern and told them they should consult him, one man flared, "What right have you to speak up? You've only been ordained three years."

I retorted on that principle, "Why don't you consult Father Bob, who has been ordained four times as long as you have?"

Finally, they did decide to consult him. When I told him the next morning, he appreciated my loyalty, and this cemented our friendship for life. I was unaware at this time how really competitive many priests are. Often they are not willing to support their peers. This is still strange to me, because I would assume that we are all working for the same cause: to establish the kingdom of God.

One of the greatest gifts Father Bob gave me was in urging me to go from door to door evangelizing, a practice I have pursued all my life. Through taking the census, as he called it, he made me more aware of some of the walls the Church had erected around its people. The Catholic Church in America, because the country was not predominantly Catholic, had to construct and maintain its walls with care. For example, intermarriage with non-Catholics even today is sometimes forbidden, if not by the Church at least by family patriarchs and matriarchs who fear what the Church thinks. In my own family, my father's brother could not get over the fact that one of his nephews was actually going to marry a non-Catholic. In looking back, I think, *what stupidity.* She turned out to be one of the best wives in the family. As a good member of the Catholic Church, however, my uncle followed this narrow mindset to a T, also believing that in intermarriages the spouse must become Catholic or at least agree that all the offspring be baptized and reared Catholic. Certainly this was thought to be a good guarantee that there would be no open rebellions that might question true faith. In going from door to door evangelizing, however, I frequently heard and hear still from one or the other spouse, "I used to be Catholic but . . . the way the Church treated my husband [wife] caused me to drop out." In America the Catholic Church has the largest membership of any church. But due to this narrow mindset, the second-largest membership in the United States is of lapsed Catholics.

For example, in my eightieth year I encountered a young Catholic lady who told me her father suggested if her husband-to-be, a strict Lutheran, would not turn Catholic, then she should become Lutheran. And she did. At first I was a little amazed, until I learned the father who advised her to do this had married a strict Catholic and because she wouldn't turn Lutheran he had turned Catholic. His idea, which he emphatically stated, was, "Two religions in a family is not good." He felt, and I can't usually disagree, some sort of compromise should be worked out if possible. Strange to say, out of his five children the Lutheran girl is the only one who attends church. You can take that for what it is worth, but I think unless we priests get more in contact with what is going on out there in the real world not only in regard to intermarriage but also concerning other issues, we are going to have more and more lapsed Catholics. Already Father Bob, for example, was much more understanding about birth control than some of the priests of his time. He believed that birth control should not be a dominant issue in the confessional. And he warned me to "go easy on the birth controllers."

Not to be apodictical, I think maybe my experience has been a bit different from many priests because Father Bob in 1945 in Kokomo taught me that the only way to know your Catholic people is to take up a door-to-door census. This is not to say (which he told me and I have certainly learned since that time) that you are converting large numbers of people, but at least you become acquainted with your own Catholic people and can begin a process of helping those who have left the Church because of ill treatment or what they perceived as ill treatment.

Because our whole country has so many people whose beliefs differ but whose religion is still centered on Christ, perhaps what we could only wish before 1960 now because of Vatican II could become a reality. Someday we could be giving communion to Protestants!

But our Church's desire for order is still strong, and one thing I gleaned from knowing Father Bob was that a man who is so different from the norm in a system that desires conformity over integrity, even a man of the stature of my pastor, is never held in high esteem by his peers. To those peers Father Bob was always either "too old-fashioned" or "not traditional enough." He insisted on holding himself to a higher standard of personal behavior than that of his peers and to them was "not human enough." He would lay himself on the line, and he was thought foolish. It seems that is the kind of self-sacrifice a priest cannot avoid if he reads the Gospel. And the response of the world around him was also similar to the responses received by our Lord, both good and bad.

I was content in Father Bob's parish, had no strong desire to leave, but our diocese, being small and less urbane than some of the larger ones, had difficulty attracting and keeping priests. Also, we had fewer priests than most other dioceses. That was the reason that after only six years I was about to become a pastor. When the word went out, one of my good friends in the diocese of Fort Wayne complained, "Hey, Red, how did you get to be a pastor after six years when we have to wait seventeen?"

I told him, "The bishop recognizes superior talent when he sees it." Of course this was said in jest, although I would like to think it was my skill and devotion and exceptional talent. I would like to think that, but I know otherwise.

Whatever the case, after only six years as an associate, I became pastor of St. Anne's parish in Monterey, Indiana. A proud moment. I became a pastor and I got my first automobile. I feel awkward now, remembering how hard I prayed for a car. In 1948 all cars were scarce, and I would hardly be high on the list of those waiting for a vehicle. Then there was money. I had hardly any. Still, *Please, God, you know how bad I need a car.*

God knew, I am sure, and so did the pastor of the parish I was leaving. I came back from church one evening and found the answer to my prayers. A doctor in Kokomo was sitting on the front porch of the rectory with Father Bob. The doctor was getting himself a new car, he said, and he offered to give me a deal on his old one. I became the owner of a $1,300 eight-year-old Mercury. When I arrived in Monterey, in all humility, it was hard not to think I had indeed arrived.

5

Trying the Waters

It was in Monterey that I had a car and, more important, the privilege of choosing a housekeeper. Well now, in truth, my mother, Luella, chose me and stayed with me in that position for thirty years. Luella and I were received with warmth I have seldom seen in the Church. St. Anne's itself was much smaller than many of the churches built at that time, but it was quite adequate for the size of the congregation, which still today numbers only about 324. It was a brick church with a wide Roman arch entrance and a steeple that was one of the landmarks of the surrounding area. The St. Anne's congregation greeted us with a reception that revealed the genuine love I always found in that congregation. It was here that all the things I had been privileged to learn thus far could be put into practice. Monterey had a school and three nuns and was more like an assignment for an experienced pastor on his second or third assignment than a parish for a novice. I truly felt blessed and intended to work as hard as I could to deserve such a rich opportunity.

Since Monterey was only forty-five miles from Notre Dame, I also had the privilege of continuing the studying there I had begun earlier during my years at Elwood and I was able to complete my master's degree in liturgy. Although Vatican II was still ahead, fortunately the religious women and St. Anne's congregation were open to changes and my studies were not in vain. We discussed the liturgy, the new possibilities in the postwar Church—all the things I had never had an opportunity to enjoy exploring in a parish.

My entry at Monterey came at the conclusion of one of the university's summer school sessions and Fr. Godfrey Diekmann, one of the greatest pioneers in the liturgy, asked me if he might spend a few days with me instead of a making the long journey back to his home base in Collegeville, Minnesota. I was delighted, not only to have his company but especially since he would have to come right back the following Sunday. Also, I knew that if I got him to speak to our congregation, it would be a positive experience for everyone, especially since I wanted to begin an active participation of the people in the liturgy of the Church. At that time the nuns had returned to Monterey for another school year, so I scheduled a parish meeting in the basement of the church for one of the evenings Father Godfrey was going to be with us.

During the supper preceding the meeting, the nun in charge of the music at Monterey commented, "Liturgical music is a good idea but impossible in the average parish." She reflected the opinion of most people, even most of the priests at Notre Dame. Remember at this time in 1948 Mass was still in Latin. The general thought was that the liturgy was just the rubrics: the red passages in the Missal and the Breviary. Father Godfrey changed this congregation's minds.

In introducing him, I spent twenty minutes telling them how great a liturgist he was. While he joshed with me about my intro, I was speaking the truth. During his dynamic talk, he had parishioners spellbound. He even cast a spell on the nun in charge of music. Knowing he had an excellent singing voice, she asked him if he would *try* to teach the people to sing responses or perhaps the Kyrie Eleison. He taught the audience not only responses and the Kryrie but also the Gloria, the Sanctus, and the Agnus Dei. What a start he got us off to! What would have taken me the whole six years I had in this parish he did in one session.

Monterey was really an experiment for me in a lot of ways. It became a church of the future without my having to struggle to get the people to accept changes. In the backcountry, this rural parish made up of farmers considered the changes we made natural, not innovative, much less threatening. It was natural that we had evening Masses (something, of course, frowned on elsewhere), but here it was convenient, really necessary for the farmers, who needed to spend their daylight hours in the fields. In rural areas, people are more responsible for their own entertainment, so of course we tried to involve the congregation more in singing. Laity singing in a Catholic church! That was liturgical renewal and it was practical. And so, we had the opportunity in new ways to make the liturgy come alive and develop a church that was more like a community of faith than a stagnant structure. How subversive could that be? After all, these were only rural folks. Right!

And we were certainly isolated. Monterey was famous among all the priests in the diocese as a place that was impossible to find, whether to visit or to be pastor. My eight-year-old Mercury had a spotlight on it, and to get back home I'd have to stop along the road and shine it around looking for the sign: TO HASCHELL'S LUMBER YARD, MONTEREY, INDIANA in order to point my car in the right direction. One night after I had been there quite a while I couldn't find the sign and had to ask the farmer how to get to Monterey. He said, "Just go south." All I knew was that south was not up or down.

One of my predecessors at Monterey on a nasty rainy night had to get in his car and lead a visiting priest twelve miles to the nearest highway. When he came back home, he saw that the visiting priest was still following him and he had to do the trek again. When they reached the crossroads, he got out of his car and pointed; "Now you go that way."

During the summers I went to Notre Dame in that beat-up Mercury, taking with me six children so they could to learn how to put good singing and dancing into the liturgy. In fact, this little town in the country became a Mecca for people interested in the liturgy. One of those summers, a Notre Dame professor, another great liturgist, Father Vitry, was on the verge of a nervous breakdown and spent a month recuperating with my mother and me. He was a pioneer translating the Latin phrases into an English that could be sung by the children and the congregation, and he taught our children. When he went back to Notre Dame to continue his teaching there, he became a Monterey publicity agent. He was so loved by all his college-age summer school students that Father Matthis, head of the university's summer school and a great admirer of Father Vitry, acquiesced when most of those students wanted to visit Father Vitry in the little parish where he was recuperating.

One day Father Mathis arranged to bring two busloads of people from Notre Dame—priests, nuns, and laypeople to have a picnic in Monterey. To prepare two busloads of people for their experience of our little town we had signs put up: HERE IS THE SPOT WHERE FATHER VITRY FED THE BIRDS AND SPOKE TO THE ANIMALS and, on the bridge where they crossed the river ST. ANNE'S

CHURCH CLEAR ACROSS TOWN. They soon found out that "clear across town" was two city blocks. During the picnic, when I had a chance, I whispered to the priests, "The beer is in the garage on ice in the garbage cans." The nuns didn't drink beer at that time (1949–50).

These Notre Dame people became publicity agents for a Father Fred who was anxious for no publicity at all. I wasn't looking for interference from the diocese, although I thought (misthought, actually) that we were too far away from the chancery for the powers there to be too concerned. It was later I learned that the bishop knew everything I was up to.

The influence these priests and nuns and laypeople from Notre Dame had on the parishioners of St. Anne's was long-lasting. Cities are fed from small towns like Monterey, so a foundation was laid for many of our people, especially those children I took to Notre Dame, to be active in their future congregations. They became leaders in the communities wherever they settled.

One of those students recently wrote to me about the great impact those experiences she had as a child had on her whole life. With her permission, portions of her letter follow:

Dear Father Fred:
     My mother-in-law has multiple myeoloma and we are taking turns as family to take care of her at her home. She is under hospice care and we've been living out the Paschal mystery through this experience. God is good and we feel like we are being ministered to ourselves.
     I was so excited to know you are writing a life-story. My recollection about the Notre Dame summers is something like this . . . there were six of us and we went four or five summers. Two of us had to sit on stools in the back seat. I cannot brag on that Mercury; it was scary—be-

sides, I married a guy who worked for General Motors. The experience was awesome. It helped me—1. In my formation of love for liturgy—2. With body expression of praise to the Lord, and—3. By exposure to religious women and their many gifts.

That was the minor impact you had on me. The major formation during my grade school years was your practical approach to faith—like your using the English language, seeing the importance of God in everyday life. You were a "real" person, not a stuffy cleric—that set the foundation for my ongoing love for Jesus Christ as an adult. Most of all this influenced our atmosphere in our home. Bill and I believe "liturgy begins at home"—so we were very Catholic in the upbringing of our four sons. So therefore, *Father Fred,* I feel you planted a seed of faith by instilling in me as a young person the importance of being a disciple. In turn a vocation to the priesthood bore fruit in our son Michael. (I hope you put this in your book!) Bill and I are grandparents of four little girls now. Our other sons and families are living out their Baptism call to serve by being very active in their different parishes. (I hope this makes your book, too!)

May God continue to use you in your golden years to continue to minister to *all those you touch.*

Gratefully yours,
Phyllis (Zehner) McKinney

During those six years in Monterey, I became friends with folks who would continue along my path of growth for years. But often to my friends from the "outside" Monterey seemed comfortable but definitely a little old-fashioned. Among these was Fr. Tom Conley from the Archdiocese of Chicago. From the "big city," this lifelong friend has spent many years trying to make me, a small-town boy, into a gentleman. He used to visit us in the rectory, which he thought could use some updating. Evidently most of the former pastors at Monterey had felt the same way.

I had only been in Monterey for six months when the carpenter called and asked, "Aren't you going to call me down to the rectory?"

I said, " What for?"

"Well, every pastor always wants to rearrange the rectory," he said. I learned that for the last twenty-five years the idea had been to tear down the rectory and build a new one. The rectory was an old-fashioned two-story brick Victorian house with white scrollwork trim, two bedrooms up, no closets but we bought wardrobes. My mother and I thought, except for the summer kitchen that was always cold, it was the best house we had ever lived in. And we fixed that summer kitchen. The first winter there we had the carpenter put insulation on the inside and out and it was comfortable. I left there in 1954. Now, forty-seven-plus years later the rectory still stands and is quite serviceable.

It was while I was in Monterey that I had my first opportunity to travel abroad. This, too, was part of my spiritual direction. Father Damasus asked me, along with my mother and Aunt Dorothy, to accompany him not only to Italy (to Rome, of course) but also to five other countries. In Germany we saw the great Catholic places, including his own monastery of Maria Laach. We went to Switzerland, Spain, Austria. The only place Father Damasus couldn't speak the native language was Spain. That traveling that began in my first years as a priest I have continued all my life. Seeing how others live in our world has helped me understand our own people better.

Whenever I think of Monterey and I think of all the human experiences I had there, there is a bond of love that I will never get over—a soft spot forever. Monterey was one of those serendipitous experiences that many folks have the opportunity to enjoy. I guess that growth comes in the Church when people who are looking for renewal find a pregnant moment when real change is possible. I was blessed to have had that experience.

Being a spiritual father, I thought I should stay in Monterey the rest of my life. A married man doesn't abandon his kids. But in 1954 I took a week off to finish my last Notre Dame summer school class on liturgy and, when I got home, I had this letter from the bishop: "I've been trying to reach you by long distance. Call me when you get home." The bishop wanted me to go to another parish.

I pleaded with him, "I just got the church redecorated, new boilers in the school, the church painted. Can't I stay and enjoy it for one year or so?"

"You think about it and pray about it," he replied. The main reason that he told me for the move was that Monterey was too far from where the activity is in Lafayette See. "I want you to be closer," he said. So he wanted me to go to Union City, which was 125 miles from Lafayette on the Ohio–Indiana border—and Monterey was forty-five miles from Lafayette? With my mother's prodding, however, I acted like an obedient son of the Church. I called him. "I'll go."

6

Stirring the Pot

I actually liked the bishop very much. He was a pastoral bishop. I was hardly in Union City for two weeks before I recognized that God's hand was in it. I soon found out why the bishop was so insistent that I come to this parish. They needed me. Things were really a mess. They had to have a change. While my predecessor was a very good man, he was one of those priests who thought he was God. He had unilaterally decided that the public school children had to be withdrawn from the public schools and attend the parochial schools for the next five months. In his opinion, they *had* to do this in order to receive first communion with the parochial school children in May. This is one example of why there had to be a change.

And so Union City was a step further in my personal and vocational journey. Seminary had given me an experience that made me uncomfortable with the definition of the Church I found myself subject to. Elwood had reinforced my feelings of discomfort and whetted my appetite for something different. Kokomo and Monterey gave me hope that there was something better for which we could strive, and Union City would be the link between all the ferment in my life and the circumstances where I was forced and allowed to become the priest I felt being nurtured inside me all these years.

After a few weeks, I felt more confident in Union City than I had even in Monterey. I no longer went to Notre Dame with great frequency but stretched my wings and took studies in seminars and brief courses in New York and other places. I had my life enriched by study and by spiritual direction from Father Damasus, which helped me put some order and coherence in what I was doing. Most of all, I had many experiences pastoring the congregation that led to my growth and theirs.

One of my greatest fears in moving to another parish was how I could start from scratch again. Yet because of my experiences at Monterey and Notre Dame, I felt more confident in tackling a new parish. It was the reaction of the congregation at St. Mary's in Union City to a new priest, however, that gave me the most confidence. They greeted me with an open-arms welcome and a pledge to go along with anything and everything I wanted to do.

In 1954, Vatican II was still a few years ahead. Most Indiana clergy, with the exception of those at Notre Dame, were not interested in studying liturgy at this time. To them it simply meant deciding when during the Mass there should be a small bow and when a medium or profound bow. At Notre Dame the study of liturgy had to do with getting people to sing more, to take part in the Mass, to respond more. Most people before Vatican II went to Mass saying their rosaries and doing their private devotions or just daydreaming until it was all over with—letting the priest do all the work at the altar. While there was much merit in the idea of the priest standing with his back to the people, that is, it projected the concept that he was an intermediary between the people and God—at Notre Dame we had experimented with saying Mass facing the people. We had found that to be very difficult, but the contact with people enriched the relationship between the priest and the people and made the people much more aware of what was happening at the altar. They came to recognize their call to an active participation in the liturgy, to feel the reality that they are part of the people of God. Pope Pius XI in 1925 said, "The faithful learn more by their active participation in the most solemn and holy mysteries of our religion exemplified in the liturgy than they do by the most solemn pronouncements of the Holy See." It is far more effective to look into the congregation than to mumble with our backs to them. And one of the things I can look back on with joy is that in three parishes—Monterey, Union City, and Remington—I had prepared the people to accept the Vatican II changes, particularly their participation during Mass with the priest facing the congregation, the Mass in English, and the singing. I had accustomed them to be active participants instead of passive spectators.

This was certainly the case in Union City. The church organist was one of the nicest, most cooperative persons I have encountered (typical priest comment). She was really delighted with the idea of the congregation singing, with the new songs, and even with my ideas of the new liturgy. The fact that she was from one of the most active and respected families in the parish also helped influence others to accept changes. The whole congregation was soon willing to be involved in the Masses. Thanks to my training at Notre Dame, we had many ways to experiment meaningfully with the liturgy. We sang—hymns, alleluias. We had lay readers who read in English while I recited in Latin. One of the best lay leaders I have ever had, Norman, read the epistle with the fervor and warmth of the Holy Spirit. You could tell Norman loved every word he said. He was a leader in the parish not only in his reading during the liturgy but also in every

66

other regard. He was the first president of the first pastoral council we had.

In a recent contact with Norman, he reminded me of the stunt he pulled one Sunday when we had a group of men from the Knights of Columbus visiting the church. (It was and still is the custom for some of these societies to go as a body to visit other churches.) Norman had suggested (or maybe I suggested) that while he was sitting in the same pew with some of these men, he would whisper to them, "Dare me to read the epistle out loud in English while Father reads it in Latin at the altar?"

And of course they said, "No. Absolutely not. Don't do that." But then as I began the epistle from the altar, loud and clear Norman started reading it in English. The men were horrified. They were not aware that I had established this as a weekly custom.

Pioneer efforts such as these were necessary to bring about much-needed changes, and as in Monterey, the children helped lead the adults. Because Norman was such a good reader, it was relatively easy for him to read in English what I was speaking in Latin. To have the main introductory parts of the Mass, such as the introit, offertory, Sanctus, and communion, verse sung in English, however, was not so simple. Yet St. Mary's children learned to sing these parts in English and the people began to have a much better grasp of what the Mass was about. This sort of experimentation I like to believe helped the people accept the transition to the whole Mass in English that Vatican II brought about. The enthusiasm these children had for the new songs and the new liturgy inspired the adults to appreciate the changes in the Mass much more.

In Union City I developed strong ties with lay leaders in ways that went beyond informal control by the purse strings of the locally powerful. I involved the laity in the discussion of what the Church was and what it was doing. In fact, I ran into trouble in every parish I was in after my experiences in these two rural parishes of Monterey and Union City due to my ignoring the powerful people of those subsequent parishes. The leaders of the later parishes welcomed me with arms around my shoulder, assuring me, "Father, we are behind you one hundred percent." Translation: "As long as you do what we say and think." But despite the occasional protest, in all my parishes I have always focused on involving people in the celebration of the Mass. The more they feel a part of the religious celebrations of the Church, the more the Church is able to help them through tragedies, which inevitably arise in life.

Let me give two examples. On one Sunday afternoon in January as I was going to go out the door of the manse, the phone rang and I learned two of Norman's boys had just drowned in an irrigation channel. The boys, nine and eleven, had picked the one spot in the channel where the drainage from the fields had flowed in to make it deeper and deeper. Anyplace else they could have walked right out of the creek. They couldn't swim; neither could their father. He had to get somebody to tie a rope around him so they could pull him out as he recovered his sons. Thank God as the only priest in town I was available. If there is any time a pastor is needed it is crisis situations such as this. And it was good that the congregation through the changes in the liturgy had a better understanding of their religion so that through the Grace of God they could be of real comfort to the grieving family.

This is one of the toughest challenges with which a priest has to deal. He must have the love expressed in a faith-filled ministry. Two sources have helped me in dealing with such tragedies: one, the suffering and tragedies I have experienced in my own family, and second, and probably more important, the spiritual direction I have received from Fr. Damasus Winzen and others throughout my life. The main reason I wanted to become a priest was to help people through these kinds of tragedies.

My second example of the importance of people understanding their faith occurred the same day. When I finally got home from anointing the boys at the edge of the creek and doing what I could to console Norman's family, my mother said, "Nick called. He's emotionally and physically exhausted. Go down and see him and comfort him." His seventy-five-year-old wife had been very ill and had died about midnight that night. Nick's response in dealing with the funeral arrangements for his wife illustrates how people who are filled with faith can rise to meet any tragedy. He wondered whether he could have the funeral on Tuesday. I said, "We could have two funerals in one day," and told him of Norman's tragedy.

"Oh, no," he said. "We'll have Jessie's Wednesday." He came to the boys' funeral and put his arms around Norman and his wife. They went to his wife's.

Whether at twenty-one or eighty-one handling these kinds of problems is always difficult, yet it's in these areas I believe I am most effective in giving spiritual direction. While I was in Union City, I can remember at least two other situations where I feel my ministrations helped.

I had for years had a clogged nasal passage and on the advice of a parishioner sought help from an ear, nose, and throat specialist in Richmond, Dr. Tom Shields. He solved my problems and we became great friends and golfing partners. Tuesday afternoons he quit at three o'clock and I would drive the few miles from Union City to join him on the course. We often had discussions about religion, but although his wife was an ardent Catholic, Tom had few religious convictions.

Some four or five years into our acquaintance I received a desperate call from his wife: "Tom needs to see you."

"Fine," I said. "Have him come over."

"He can't. He's too ill for that, Father. Can you come here?"

Of course I went right over. When I got there, Tom was sitting helpless in a chair like a little boy. He had recognized that he had hit bottom. His wife had finally convinced him that he had to deal with the addictions that he realized were threatening his life and his marriage. He told me in a pleading voice, "I want to take instructions and join the Catholic Church."

I knew Tom's aversion to the authoritarianism of the Catholic Church, and I said, "Let's investigate what the Church teaches and then you can make a decision."

"Father Fred," he replied, "now I am confused. I have been struggling with this for a long, long time. I have made up my mind. I want to join the Church. I don't want to investigate."

Although at the time I didn't realize how desperate the situation was, I began giving him instruction immediately, and I learned almost as much as he did. He went after his instructions in the Church much as he went after his study of medicine and his golf game. We would play golf until you almost had to make the last putt in the dark.

As he recovered his health, he became, in his words, "a much better husband, a much better father of their two children, a much better doctor—and a much better golfer." Often on the golf course he would tell me, "It's so

70

much easier to live life more fully and productively when you are depending on God and not just on yourself." What a profound statement. We remained friends for the rest of his life, and I still am friends with his wife. She has said to me many times that because of my being his friend and bringing him into the Church I was God's instrument in giving him twenty more years to live. I have always answered, "No, Mom Shields, you're the one who gets the credit." And she is. She gave him the love he needed to turn his life about.

I may have been an instrument that brought Tom back to health, but he reciprocated by sending me people who needed spiritual help rather than merely medical. And through him I met Dr. Joseph Quigley, who became another lifelong friend and another person I feel I helped with my spiritual directions.

Tom said to me one day, "Father, I want you to go see a man who was in very bad car accident a few days ago." Tom said he had witnessed the accident. He told me that the man's wife had died and the medical team thought surely the man himself would die. They wanted to ship him to Indianapolis, but Tom had said, "You are not moving that man. It would kill him."

He had literally saved Joe Quigley's life. Tom told me a young priest from Indianapolis had anointed Joe, but that he needed to talk.

I said, "OK, Tom, I'm available." So I stopped at the hospital. I had to wait a whole hour or more even to see him. When I went in I said, " Joe, Doctor Tom wanted me to stop by and see you, thought you might want to go to confession."

This man, who was lying there practically dying, did, as Tom said, need to talk and talk he did for almost an hour.

71

I said, "You don't have to tell me all the stuff."

He said, "Father, I have to tell you."

As I listened to him I realized the truth of Doctor Tom's insight.

Joe told me of the struggle he had had with his wife and mother and his animosity toward others. And when he was finished ridding himself of what was troubling him, the healing process began. I've often thought since that psychic or soul healing has to take a more prominent place in recovering health.

Joe from that moment on, I think, began to live. He got rid of all that was troubling him. He had an entirely different and positive attitude as he struggled to recover, to live and to walk again. It's just one instance that had proved to me the validity of my lifelong emphasis on the need for spiritual direction as it can be given and received in the confessional. Joe became another lifelong friend. We played golf together and he helped this "lad least likely to succeed" to become a more mature human being by showing me how to overcome one of the great weaknesses of my life—public speaking. He pointed out to me how muddled I was in my thinking—particularly in the pulpit. Obviously, it wasn't my homilies that had inspired people. So if I have succeeded in helping other people through critical periods, I have been richly rewarded time and time again by their helping me become a more effective priest.

As I look back in my eighties on some of the these incidents I can understand a remark I still occasionally hear, but not near as blatantly as it was in the past: "Father, you're a muddled mess in your thinking, but your sincerity and charismatic style cover a multitude of sins."

About the same time as these tragedies and near-tragedies occurred another somewhat lighter incident happened that points up the necessity for the Church and its clergy to present the faith in a way that all can feel the Love of God. Bob, a man from a neighboring parish, came to ask me if I could do anything to help him cope with a family problem. (His coping skills were never the greatest.) I was able to help him a little with this, his latest problem, and he told me he'd about decided to move into our parish. I wasn't thrilled. I already knew this character from a neighboring pastor and from some visits I had had with him earlier. He was a very difficult man, although in his way he tried to be very good man.

He had first come to see me because on a Christmas day his pastor was out of town and he wanted someone to give last rites to his mother. Too, he had come to see me because he didn't like his own pastor. (There were few people he really did like.) I had left my Christmas dinner cooling on the table to drive over and give his mother last rites. Later, after his mother died and was buried, he and his wife came to thank me for being with the mother. The way he talked down to his wife during this visit, however, irritated me no end, and I really dressed him down. Later his wife, who had a habit of filling me in on things after the fact, told me, "Father Fred, your dressing my husband down and sticking up for me cost you one hundred dollars." He had come over with the idea of making some kind of monetary contribution for my several trips to his mother.

I told her, "That's OK. I would still do it again." I had long ago made a vow never to let money interfere with my ministry. Despite all my uncomfortable encounters with Bob, I have to admit I liked this unlikable man. He did move to our parish and when we started parish pastoral councils, I advised those forming our council to include him on it. Pastors should not surround themselves just with yes-people. I thought this curmudgeon filled the bill as a son of a gun and the council as well as I needed him as a died-in-the-wool "no" man. When we had our meetings, he countered all of our ideas and there were times when either I or others felt like saying to him, "Bob, why be difficult? With just a little more effort you could be absolutely impossible."

After he had been on the council for a couple of years, I was asked to a move to Remington. Bob totally surprised me. He insisted that the council get the parish to buy me a new car to leave town. They did. A brand-new Chevrolet 700. I had repainted my beat-up Mercury. Although it was about twenty years old, I still loved the old heap and I was glad, nearly my last day in town, when I found someone who needed it. A poor man starting a business had had one of his two junk cars go out, and I gave him my old car. He and his partner were delighted and so was I.

I later learned again from Bob's wife the explanation for his generosity on my behalf. She gave me the inside scoop—he was so elated that some priest had finally recognized his superior talents and asked him to be on the parish council that he wanted to show his gratitude.

Incidentally, my mother/housekeeper, Luella, was overjoyed at getting rid of the old Mercury. Not long after I got the new Chevrolet, I had to preside at a funeral in a neighboring town and asked her if she would like to drive while I made some notes for the service. I was sitting in the backseat jotting down ideas oblivious to what was going on when suddenly she screamed, "Oh my God, oh my God!"

Afraid we were about to have an accident, I dropped my papers, leaned forward and said, "Mother, what's the matter?"

"I was going one hundred miles per hour," she gasped, clutching the steering wheel. The old Mercury never had had much power and Mother had a heavy foot.

But to finish the story about Bob. Not surprisingly for Bob, he totally disliked the pastor who took my place in Union City. During the first year of this pastor's ministry, Bob never put a dime in the collection basket. So it was that after I was in Remington only from June to January the head of the Remington pastoral council said, "Father, we've got something to show you." He took me around to the front of the church to see a brand-new Pontiac.

I said, "I don't understand."

"Well, Father, one of your friends from a previous parish came around and convinced the head of our council who owned a car dealership that you needed a new car." It was Bob again.

And, of course later, I found out from his wife that whole story. Because he hadn't given a dime to his parish, his conscience had bothered him, so he came to Remington and drove a hard bargain with that council.

"What cash would it take to trade in Father's car for a new one?" he asked. I don't know what the reply was, but I do know he said, "Here is three hundred dollars. You people can certainly make up the rest."

That was the amount he would have given to the parish he belonged to except he didn't like the pastor.

I told the council chairman, "If he comes back next year tell him I need an airplane."

My fond memories of Union City aren't confined to my relationships with parishioners or my mother's peccadilloes; the clergy, too, gave me some trying moments and some good laughs.

For most my years in Union City, our diocesan bishop

was a man originally from Brooklyn. He later became a cardinal, John Joseph Cardinal Carberry. The first time he came for a confirmation, he asked a priest familiar with the area, Monsignor Ward, how to get to our little town, how far it was from Lafayette.

Monsignor Ward told him, "Oh, Bishop, it's just a couple hours' drive." What was omitted in this conversation was that Monsignor Ward seldom traveled less than eighty miles an hour while Bishop Carberry's top speed was fifty miles an hour and he wasn't used to rural roads. So allowing two hours to get to our town, he arrived an hour and fifteen minutes late.

That was only the beginning of a weekend that was a total fiasco. My friend Father Francis was there also for the confirmations. As he was the only priest in his parish, it had been a struggle for him to complete an assignment the bishop had given him. For over a period of several months he had attended weekly meetings on the rules and regulations peculiar to our midwestern diocese. And he had written a book, a comprehensive book, on those midwestern guidelines. He had told me on several occasions how wonderful this bishop from Brooklyn now in Indiana was, how lucky we were to have him. But on the day he came to my place for confirmation, he had received a copy of the book that he had supposedly compiled. He recognized none of it and after a few phone calls learned that our new bishop had just copied all the rules and regulations from the eastern diocese. Father Frank didn't mind that the bishop wanted to use the eastern diocesan rules, but he was furious that he had been asked to make all those trips, attend all those meetings, spend all that time writing—for nothing.

I had always heard about Frank's terrible temper. Now I experienced it. Supper was supposed to have been at five o'clock, and Frank was going to have a little drink before dinner. But the later it got as we waited for the bishop, the more Frank drank, and the more he drank the angrier he got and the more he swore. He could swear for twenty-five minutes without repeating himself. I rather enjoyed it, except it was in my house and the pious ladies, one of them a recent convert, were there preparing the gourmet meal for His Excellency the Bishop. My biggest concern was to try to shut all the doors and windows so the sound wouldn't get to the kitchen. Somehow or other we got Frank to shut up just as the bishop finally arrived at 6:45.

But the travail wasn't over. We ate a hurried supper and got to church ready to go out on the altar when the electricity went off. The bishop couldn't make any decisions unless he first made a nine-day novena. He couldn't figure how we could possibly have confirmation. So I had to step in and make the decisions. We did it by candlelight. The lights never came back on. It was a beautiful candlelight service. Little did I realize, however, that we were going to have candlelight the next two nights in the new neighboring parishes.

The second night a storm broke again and electric power lines were down over the highway, so state troopers were directing drivers to the narrow country side roads, which were difficult and dangerous at best and now seemed to have a fast-flowing river on either side. I'm sure Father Frank was somewhat comforted that we had been able to introduce our new bishop to the Midwest. And I'm sure the bishop was glad eventually to escape from our wilderness.

On another occasion, when the bishop stayed at my house as a convenient place while he had business over at this far foreign end of his diocese, he had a confrontation with a great missionary priest from abroad, Father Pete. Father Pete was one of the finest priests we have ever had. He singlehandedly inaugurated and taught others like myself the practice of visiting and serving the migrant population. He understood the mindset these people had in many of their practices. To them, it was necessary to be married first by the Justice of the Peace, and then by the Padre. On one occasion, I had done all the paperwork necessary to witness such a marriage in the Church and arranged a date for the ceremony, but for some reason, the couple wanted to have it on a holiday two days later (Labor Day). In my meticulousness over rules and regulations, I wondered, *Suppose they sleep together.* When I spoke to them about the matter, the man said, "That's all right, Padre. I'll make my wife sleep under the bed for a few days." I mention this incident because Father Pete broadened my vision of the apostolate considerably. Being from another culture, he had a grasp of things different from mine. "In Mexico," he told me, "it isn't at all unusual for the couple to be married by the state and not get married by the priest until years later—and our idea that they are living in sin is ridiculous."

I know I wasn't asked to move to Remington because of my shenanigans in Union City. In truth, I thought that my being 125 miles away from Lafayette kept the chancery unaware of my activities in Union City. There were no spoken objections to my experiments with the liturgy, but the bishop who succeeded Bishop Carberry quickly heard about and did get upset when he learned I was present at a marriage between a Catholic and a Methodist. He called me in and asked, "How could you possibly be present at this invalid union of a Catholic and a Protestant in the Protestant Church?"

I looked him right in the eye and said, "Because it was the only human and Christian thing to do."

All he said was "Oh?" after I had explained that the bridegroom had said if they were married in the Catholic Church the children would be raised Protestant and if they got married in the Protestant Church they could be raised Catholic. Reason enough I felt for me to be there. Today I could have participated legitimately. There's that rebellion in me the rector of St. Meinrad's sensed in my years in the seminary. To me, it's just that it makes more sense to do what makes more sense.

I felt comfortable with my small rebellions in Union City. That little parish, I think, was the ideal setting for a growing love affair with a liturgy that would include the whole people of God. I was experiencing Church even as I was in the process of working to change the Church. I had my small Vatican II experiences even as the larger Church was in ferment, waiting for the guiding hand of a Pope named John. In Logansport, my next parish, Vatican II was an accomplished fact.

7

Opening the Windows

If I was engaged in something akin to a small revolution in Monterey and Union City, then Remington/Wolcott and Logansport, Indiana, were my Lexington and Concord. In Monterey I felt as if I should be pastor and spiritual father there for the rest of my life. But since moving on to other parishes, I have realized that it is important for pastors to move about. It challenges the pastor and the people.

I was received very warmly in Remington/Wolcott, just as I was in Monterey and Union City. Shortly after I arrived, I was visited by a good friend, Fr. Leonard Kostka, C.PP.S (that's Congregation of the Precious Blood—not the Catholic Pickpocket Society, as St. Joseph College students used to call it). Father Kostka told me, "Fred, all you need to do here is make the Sign of the Cross and say three Hail Marys and you're *in*." He was jesting, but he meant what he said, because the priest I was following had done virtually nothing. It's been my fortune or misfortune often to follow priests who have left messes to clean up. You remember if the pastor I followed in Union City had insisted that all the children who wanted to make their first communion would have to withdraw from the public school from January to May.

Fortunately, the priest in Remington had done a

wonderful job of redecorating the church, Sacred Heart. He had the whole physical plant in good order. But he didn't do much spiritually. He was very demanding in the pulpit, but not so much on faith issues as on monetary issues. Himself a gambler and cardplayer, he found a number of ways to enrich the parish and himself. One of the young parishioners told me that this priest had blessed every home and every farm every spring. I had done the same thing in Union City, so I couldn't see what the problem was until the young man said, "It cost us twenty-five dollars to get our fields blessed. Both my father and I gave the priest ten dollars, and my brother's wife gave five dollars." In the sixties, twenty-five dollars was a pretty steep charge for a three-minute blessing. One of the parishioners told me the priest usually stayed for dinner, too. We shouldn't have to be paid extra every time we turn around. I think part of the trouble in churches today is the overemphasis on money. Father Bob in Kokomo told me that he almost always returned money given to him for any sacramental ministry. For example, at baptisms he would tell the parents to use the money they offered him to start the baby's bank account. His one exception was when the owner of one of the big factories in town gave him a one hundred dollar bill. He took it. The factory owner would have been offended if he hadn't. He was a member of one of the families in Kokomo who "ran the church."

There are generally a few families in every parish who "run the church." Sometimes they monopolize the priest's time, but most often they are helpful. Art Sego was the first man to welcome me to Remington. He helped me as he had helped every pastor before me and, in a nice gentle way, handed out good advice. The best thing of all was that just as I was used to in Union City, Art was a eucharistic minister who was already reading the epistle in English while the pastor read it in Latin. I'll have to say that's one good practice the former pastor had introduced.

Sacred Heart parish was started on the path to change, but they weren't very far along. Their conservativeness was much greater than that in Union City and was a real challenge. It was here in Remington/Wolcott and later in Logansport, however, that I finally had the support of the Church in doing more fully the things that Vatican II recommended. And I was more assured. I became less frightened at the common objection: "Father, we have never done that before." I was enthusiastic. I had wanted to and did make some of the changes in the liturgy in Monterey and Union City long before Vatican II made it the official program of the Church. In spite of my being isolated in those towns that were the farthermost points of the diocese, word of my innovations got around. And frankly, I considered the uncomplimentary remarks of a good priest friend and neighbor to be complimentary. He frequently swore at me, usually in jest but with some element of irritation, "God damn you, Schroeder, you and a few other nuts are responsible for these changes." Let's face it—the whole Catholic Church was in a rut and it took a few of us innovators to wake everyone up.

It was here in Remington/Wolcott that I began consciously and legitimately to put into practice the changes of Vatican II. All local parishes are a fertile field for the Holy Spirit to work in, even those as conservative and resistant to progress as these were. Don't get me wrong; these were lovely folks, independent folks. It is just that they were lost in the thirties or, for some of the more advanced, perhaps the early fifties.

Remington/Wolcott was a prosperous farming community of something over a thousand folks, with many of the participants in the church living on farms outside of the town itself. One of the claims to fame that marked the community was the fact that during the Depression the Remington bank had been the only one in the area not to close. The community hated change. It viewed with almost horror the lawlessness of the young in protesting the Vietnam War. Therefore, it was amusing but not really out of character that when the state mandated school consolidation and they were told to unite with a twin school six miles away, the parents lay down in front of the school bus. Change! When a Remington colleague, a Presbyterian minister, and his wife adopted a biracial child, half black and half white, it was discovered that Remington still had a statute on the books prohibiting any black person from being inside the city limits after dark. No one suggested that the baby leave town, but then, neither did anyone feel it important to eliminate the statute. Change! So it would appear that if a priest seriously wanted to innovate, Remington/Wolcott was hardly the ideal environment in which to begin. But as they say, timing is everything and the times sometimes thrust opportunities on us that we either take advantage of or let pass forever.

When I think back on some of the things that happened in Remington/Wolcott and later in Logansport, I am sure that I was far more reactive than proactive. I did not plan to do the things I did; it just seems that the moments demanded something and that is what I did. Translation by some of the priests and other laity would be, "Fred did exactly what he wanted to do when he wanted to do it regardless of the consequences." I did do what I wanted to do—no doubt about it—but it was because I was so happy to discover that what I had thought all along the Church ought to be doing had become the official policy of the Church. All the effort I had expended on educating myself on the Church's liturgy coupled with the new concept that the Church is all the people of God gave me hope these ideas could be validated and accepted by the whole ecclesiastical Church.

I realized if the half-formed vision of a Church that took advantage of its whole constituency and afforded respect to every part of the body was to come about, there were several things that had to occur:

First, the laity would have to be educated as to the theological justification of taking their *rightful place* as partners with the clergy. They had to be trained in the implementation of the possibility.

Second, we needed to recognize the wonderful opportunities that we had to work together ecumenically for a common goal.

Finally, in order to change the status quo, we needed to risk criticism or even hostility from those who represented the most power in the congregations. It is very important to gain credibility with the youth, the ostracized, and those who might be the agents of change or the source of renewal in the Church of tomorrow. While I am sure such thoughts were never set down in any orderly fashion (especially by Fred—orderly I have never been), the things I did, the programs I initiated, the partnerships into which I entered seemed to indicate that this is certainly where I was coming from.

And I had good support from the diocese. Thank God our newly elected Bishop Gallagher got in the final and most important sessions of Vatican II in 1965. He came home alive with enthusiasm. He as well as many of his clergymen were excited about the revolution that Vatican II opened for us priests and laypeople, but hardly anyone was aware of where these changes might lead. The bishop had scheduled study days for himself with the clergy to see where the solemn pronouncements might lead in the life of the ordinary person in the pew whose sole task up to this time had been to pay, pray, and obey.

And I scheduled study days for the congregation. I had arrived in the farming community of Remington/Wolcott in the late fall and winter, a time when farm work was a little less demanding. So it was possible for us to have many educational meetings in our church basement. Farmers are strong-headed people, and they were not really open to the changes that Vatican II was proposing. So what I tried to do during the long winter months to bring Bishop Gallagher's educational process to the ordinary people in the church basement.

You can take that both literally and figuratively. The basement was a good place for friendship, evangelization, community building—and, therefore, for discussing all the changes that now were somehow to find their expression in a well-orchestrated liturgy in our own language, the priest facing the people instead of the wall, and the people once again taking their legitimate part in the celebration of the liturgy.

This was no easy task for clergy or for the people. When the payoff time came, we no longer had a choice: the Mass *was* going to be in the language of the people and they *were* going to take their part in the reading and singing. Our people in the community paid me a compliment. They said it wasn't so difficult for them because we had had all those meetings in the basement, the church social hall. They had been through the process of education and acceptance needed before this became the official pattern.

They would pick up from all the neighboring parishes

stories of horrible stubborn rebellions against these changes. To put it in some of the language of the farmers, "Ah, shucks, Father, you prepared us so we can accept these changes a lot easier than our neighbors." Neighboring priests had told their congregations they didn't like the changes themselves, but they had to do what the Bishop and the Pope said regardless. Isn't that great motivation?

I had good help in preparing the people. John Egan, a professor at St. Joseph's, helped me to introduce changes in the music. A good Catholic, married with eight kids, he was very ecumenical. Father Bierberg called John the true Renaissance man. He loved to come to Remington to play and sing one or two Masses, sometimes bringing choirboys with him.

And as usual, Art Sego was a great help to me as we prepared the people for the changes. And it was he who helped me meet clergy of other faiths. In many small towns the only lodge service organization is either the Lion's Club or the Elk's. There often is no K of C. Art got me to join the Lion's Club, and through it I developed good rapport with people of all faiths and even became good friends with a man who was known throughout the countryside as a Catholic basher. He called himself Corncob Dickie, and like Art and me his last name began with S. The three of us became warm friends and called ourselves the Triple S. We joked together about buying and selling used corncobs. But we got some serious business done, too.

A big issue in the town was daylight saving time. If different members of a family were operating on different times, it would have been hard on everybody, even the cows, who were used to being milked at the same time morning and evening. Dad would be going to work on one time and the kids on another time, making it rough especially for housewives. With help from my Lion's Club friends, I managed to persuade most of my congregation and others in the town that we should go along with the rest of Indiana on daylight savings time.

While I had Lion's Club, which let me meet people of other faiths, my mother also went out of her way to become friends with people of all faiths. She had her hair done in Louise's Beauty Parlor. Louise, who lived down the alley from our church, was a member of another Christian church. She'd tease me if I walked through her alley to go the block and a half to downtown. "I'm sorry, Reverend Father, " she'd say. "This is a private alley." Of course it wasn't and we had great fun over it.

I had parishioners, too, with strong ecumenical feelings. The most vocal was a veterinarian whom we called the Martin Luther of the parish. In this still ultraconservative community we needed a Martin Luther. He objected to some of the Catholic attitudes and practices still in force at that time despite Vatican II: such as you had to be a Catholic to get to heaven; you shouldn't marry anyone who wasn't Catholic; you should never go into anybody else's non-Catholic church during a service, even for a baptism or a wedding in that church.

With that mentality you can imagine what a scandal it was when Father Fred went to visit Protestant churches and at times even took part in the services. My last Mass was at 10:00 A.M. If it ended at 11:00 or sooner I would rush down two blocks to Rev. Craig Meyers's church, pen and pencil in hand to listen to his homilies and take notes. Years later Presbyterians from Remington/Wolcott still tell me, "Father, you have no idea what that did for some of us to see you as a Catholic churchman do what you risked doing." I had not seen it as a risk.

I was asked during this time to give a talk at the Chautauqua. A Chautauqua is anything but a Catholic affair. The title of my talk was "The Gospel Is Ecumenism." It was so well received that four presbyteries in the northern half of Indiana wanted me to give the same talk in their respective areas. Invariably I was told, "Father, you'd make a good Presbyterian minister—*and* you could get married!"

By no means was I the only Catholic "pioneer" in our area. Some of the priests from St. Joseph's College and surrounding towns would meet together with Protestant clergy at the college. On one occasion while discussing the word *Protestant* as protesting the practices of the Catholic Church, one of the Protestant clergy emphasized that protestation isn't the main emphasis any longer. "Is there anyone here of the clergy who would call themselves Protestant in the original meaning of the word?" he asked. Guess who raised his hand? Father Fred. Catholic. Got quite a laugh.

One of my own congregation told me, however, "Father, we laymen were way ahead of you priests. We never thought Protestants were all going to hell. We've gotten along with them for years. We've had to." Thank God that is true today. And today the laypeople are once again way ahead of the hierarchy.

But all of my help during these ten years didn't come from Lions or laypeople, or my Protestant friends. My good friend Father Kostka was a professor at St. Joseph's College. He became a part-time helper for me, especially on weekends. He was a wonderful homilist and had good rapport with anyone he met, and his advice to me was al-

88

ways sound. Through him I found a way to better understand and help our young people.

Because of Father Kostka and my friendship with various other priests at St. Joseph's College I was offered a chance to teach a class in religion. The department was handling an overflow crowd of freshmen that year. After the first semester, all the new students wanted to get in my class—not because I was that excellent an instructor. I couldn't hold a candle to the scholarly Father Bierberg, who taught the other class. No, they signed up for my class because I was easy. Father Bierberg would actually flunk people. I just couldn't do that. It always seemed to me that flunking somebody in religion would be equivalent to telling him or her to go to hell. I feel my instincts were valid, because not too long after my year at St. Joseph's they dropped religion as a requirement. Most of these kids had had grade school, high school, and now college religion classes. And most of the material was a repetition of what they had already learned but on a supposedly higher level. Since Remington and Wolcott were only ten miles from St. Joseph's, some of the boys from our parish went there. They had not had all the background years in religion classes, and a few found the course very interesting but very difficult. But they were in the minority.

While I can understand the student's point of view about taking the class, teaching the class was a great learning experience for me. Although my main interest had been sacramental theology and I had done my postgraduate work at Notre Dame, teaching forced me to prepare for the classes and was a refresher—for me. Two observations: Once in a while a student from my parish would become engaged to a nice young lady. If she happened not to be Catholic, the boy would bring her to me

89

and say, "Make a Catholic out of her." I generally had to insist that they come to the indoctrination of the girls. The boys were sick of religion, yet to my surprise they would tell me after the course of instructions, "I've had religion rammed down my throat since I was knee-high to a grasshopper, but I must confess this is the first time it really made sense." I'm sure it made sense because finally it was being applied to everyday life.

I didn't have just boys in class. Girls had suddenly been accepted in this all-boys school. In the first class I had only one young lady, but she lifted the whole tone of the class of sixty to seventy-five boys. Later she married one of the smartest of those boys.

I was not a success as a college teacher. My gift has always been in pastoral ministry. For me, the Vatican II changes opened a way for the power of good people in the parish whose gifts are often ignored to be combined with the new theological possibilities that opened up. They prepared the way for the whole people of God to be mobilized for service and evangelization to the whole world. And they prepared the way for the Church to work with *other* congregations for the good of all.

When I was in the Remington/Wolcott area, there were five established churches: the Roman Catholic parish I served, a United Methodist church, a Presbyterian congregation, a Christian church, and a Baptist church. All of us faced the same problems, and none of us had the power to make a maximum impact on those problems by ourselves.

One of the most immediate problems involved dealing with the local youth. They were relatively tame in comparison to the youth in more urban areas. However, they were still showing rebellion against both the restrictive practices of their elders, and, more serious, the hypocrisy they perceived in the contrast between the stated and practiced value system they were taught. In a town in which the American Legion was one of the leading institutions, the local youth and the college people who came down from St. Joseph's College in nearby Rensselaer felt alienated from the position of their elders regarding the war in Southeast Asia. The elders could not understand the young people's lack of patriotism. They often took violent exception to the "hippies and commies" (then the descriptions got downright uncomplimentary). In a town where adult and teen drinking was a norm, the argument over the relative merits of other kinds of substance that were being introduced certainly touched our area. And college kids coming home shared more than their academic educational experiences.

The question was "How does the Church speak credibly to the young about value systems we espouse while listening to challenges to the status quo that the young bring up?" Mere scolding did not work, probably never has. None of the local churches seemed to have any contact at all with the majority of kids, while the "good kids," whatever they did in private, were held up as models of what respectful, patriotic Christian kids ought to be like. Young people tend to identify themselves with the ball team or with social relationships, instead of with the church.

Yet in this small, certainly conservative community, we formed one of the first ministerial groups that included both Protestant and Catholic clergy from three towns, Remington, Wolcott, and Rensselaer. The smallness of our ecumenical group allowed us to become more than the usual "fellowship" group where everything is discussed except religion and politics. Together we advocated for the concerns of the young and interpreted their positions to the city fathers and mothers—something the young could not do for themselves given the level of volume in their conversations. We also led community worship services and established a coffeehouse in our parish hall for the whole community.

Throughout the early years of my ministry, I was afraid to discuss religion with ministers or parishioners of other faiths. (You've heard people say, probably proudly, "Two things I never discuss are religion and politics," yet those are two great governing forces in our lives.) But the interpersonal respect of these clergymen plus the commonality of our problems created a group capable of doing things others only talked about. Not only did we work together on community problems; we also established interchurch gatherings discussing what was at that time a Protestant movement toward reunion, the Consultation on Church Union. It included all the theological issues that unite as well as those that divide us within the Christian community.

All in all, Remington/Wolcott was a most unlikely place for progressive or innovative efforts to develop. It was a model that showed how much could be done in such a short time even in seemingly infertile soil if only the focus is on the Church's mission and not on making targets out of our non-Catholic peers, or vice versa. So many of the issues that face the Church today are not Catholic or Protestant issues. They are human issues. And to assume that all the answers that can help us be the Church Christ calls us to be will be Catholic or Protestant is certainly presumptuous. John XXIII said, "It's high time we open some windows and let some fresh air in." The windows that Vatican II and the world forced the Church to open were meant to bring light into our lives no matter how fearful we might be of what that light might reveal.

Most of what I tried to do in Remington/Wolcott was in reaction to needs presented by circumstances in the church and in the community. No one in our congregation, for example, was prepared or at least came forth to be a coordinator for our CCD program. My Presbyterian counterpart in Remington Rev. Craig Meyers, had a wife who had received her masters' in Christian education from McCormick Seminary in Chicago and obviously found no professional opportunity in a town the size of Remington. Why not, I thought, employ a person trained to teach and trained to teach religious curricula, even if she is not a Catholic? Mind you, in these years, in our parish, the idea was received with enthusiasm by most and grudgingly by the rest. I can't help but think the reason that this was acceptable was because whoever protested most might then be tapped for the job.

But the strangest thing occurred. The woman did a marvelous job. The children loved her. The parents were satisfied. And she taught the curricula scrupulously. If there appeared that rare instance when her own beliefs were inconsistent with what she had to teach, she would call in one of our folks to cover that particular area.

There was only one complaint. And it was so serious that it threatened to scuttle the whole enterprise. When I gave her her own parking place with her name publicly displayed, the reality, which had been acceptable, was not nearly as important as the appearance, which was a breach of order and tradition.

The beginning of these changes wrought by Vatican II seemed to be climaxed on the celebration of the Reformation, the fourth Sunday in October 1965. Our little ecumenical group planned to commemorate the occasion by an evening meeting in our Catholic church in Remington. From a diocesan meeting for Vatican II study earlier that same day in Kokomo I had brought home mimeographed sheets of the first draft of Vatican II and had posted them prominently in the vestibule of our Sacred Heart Catholic Church. When I spoke at the ecumenical meeting, I tried to be a bit humorous. While I identified them for what they were—1965 Vatican II—I said, "Really, they are very similar to Martin Luther's original document, which he had posted to the entrance of the Wittenberg Cathedral. It only took us four centuries to catch on."

When I was first ordained I thought Martin Luther was a demon straight from hell. Now I think he was one of the greatest religious reformers of all time. Luther alerted us to the problems we had in the Church that we needed first to admit and face and then do something about. There were many abuses. It led to what we call the counterreformation.

For this ecumenical meeting with five ministers of both Catholic and Protestant faiths participating, the church was packed—standing room only. All the ministers spoke. I was master of ceremonies. The minister from the Christian church opened with a long, long, long prayer; a Presbyterian minister, Reverend Meyers, preached the sermon, and another Protestant minister gave the final benediction.

This was the glorious part and the most uplifting part of my ten-year stay in this area. My heart was leaping with joy that because what we had been studying about, hoping and praying for since the early days of study at Mundelein and Notre Dame was becoming a real possibility and reality. Yet at the same time some of the ideas of Vatican II created real doubts in my own heart about my Catholic faith that hitherto I had always taken so much for granted.

8

Crisis of Faith

One of the things we Catholics had always been taught was not to doubt. If you told a religious sister you doubted, you had your wrist slapped. It's a sin to doubt. Yet all these changes helped create in me crises of faith. My spiritual director having died, I had no one I felt comfortable turning to help me with these agonizing uncertainties.

Shortly after this time, in the fall, through my contact with St. Joseph's College at Rensselaer I was privileged to be in the company of four fine Catholic priests, one of whom had even been an expert at Vatican II. One of the others was a teacher at St. Joseph's College; another was the president of our newly formed Priest's Counsel. Here, I thought, was my chance to get some help, which I badly needed. Finally I took courage and pleaded, "Holy Fathers, I need your help. I'm having serious doubts about my Catholic faith."

Instead of giving me counsel or even consolation, these priests did the same thing the nun would have done. They slapped my wrists and said, "You are not supposed to doubt." I knew that. But I was doubting.

So here there was no help for an inner turmoil that put in jeopardy my whole vocation. Then, just before Lent, Fr. Leo Piguet, the pastor at St. Thomas Aquinas,

Purdue's Newman chaplain at West Lafayette, called me up and asked if I would be a part of a group of six liberal and six conservative priests who were going to have a series of discussions on the issues in the Church that had been raised by Vatican II. The bishop was to be present as well as a trained psychologist who was good at conducting these kinds of meetings. I thought, *At last, this is my chance to get some real help.*

So as a consequence we met every Monday night during the season of Lent 1966 from 9:00 P.M. till 12:00 or even 1:00 A.M. When I would arrive home at nearly 2:00 A.M., I used to wonder what the parishioners would think if they saw me out that late. I figured I would just tell them the truth, that I was meeting with a bishop and twelve priests in Lafayette.

Those meetings were painful because as I was looking for help I appeared to others a devil's advocate. During the sessions I questioned things about the Church's stand on birth control, the power structure, the money question. Priests on both sides of the fence told me that if looks could kill, the bishop's glare would have had me dead several times. However, my life was spared because Father Leo had had the foresight to have the trained psychologist who was also an expert at communication see that there was no bloodshed. But my crisis of faith was not solved. I got to voice my concerns, but there were no reassuring responses. Maybe they were doubting, too, and wouldn't admit it.

As a consequence of these meetings Bishop Gallagher and Fr. Leo Piguet decided to extend the discussions to all the clergy in the diocese. Remember, the time right after Vatican II was a time of great turmoil dividing the clergy on whether the changes were increasing the faith or threatening it. At a retreat in June, instead of having a missionary talk to us as had been the custom in the past, one of our own diocesan priests arranged for all the opening speeches. Then we broke up into small groups and discussed matters of faith and morals, especially in the light of Vatican II. After supper the leaders of the several groups gave a report on their discussions. My report had them in stitches. I found I had a sense of humor I had never realized before.

When that was finished, each evening we had one main talk. Father Leo had asked me to give one of those talks about my crisis of faith. After supper, it took one of my priest friend's reassuring whispers to give me the courage to get up before the gathering. In introducing me Father Leo said, "Now you are going to see a different side of Father Fred, a serious side."

I found from their reactions that I wasn't the only one having doubts. I spoke of my various crises of faith and ended the talk, maybe as a sort of justification, quoting Alfred Lord Tennyson's, "There is more honest faith in one legitimate doubt than in half the world's creeds."

Father Leo is a pro at handling wild discussions. One priest who is somewhat a leader in upholding every one of the Catholic traditions objected to my doubting anything. When Father Leo would get him set down, in no time at all he would be up again. Believe me, giving my talk before all the clergy in the diocese, especially on doubting the faith, was one of the hardest things I have ever done. I wondered whether I had committed ecclesiastical suicide. That night and the next day the reactions of the clergy were most revealing. It was their remarks that were good indications of where they were. Affectionately one would say, "We'll pray for you, Father." Another, "Fred, you've lost the faith. We feel sorry for you." But others said, "Father Fred, that's the first breath of first fresh air we've heard since ordination."

In my speech, what crises did I discuss? I started out with something that was fairly easy—the realization that the Adam and Eve creation story is a myth. I had taken everything in the Bible literally. For example, I was as naive and shocked as a nun I knew who learned in a biology class that a woman *does not* have one less rib than a man. I had never been troubled before or even really noticed that the Bible has two creation accounts. I used illustrations like this to say, "The first thing you know, they'll even be doubting the Virgin birth." And subsequently, that is a disputed issue, a most agonizing one for me to even consider questioning, although a professor at St. Joseph's College who helped me write my speech, asked, "Who cares?" I cared! I felt once you start removing foundation stones of Catholic belief, the whole structure might collapse. Today one of the foremost scripture scholars, at least in the United States, Raymond Brown, has written a book about the Virgin birth. But being a theologian, he's really skirted the issue as everybody else has. Why does it matter? It made me wonder at the time if the whole Bible was just a fancy story, what we would call today a myth. Some of it is, but a lot of it is not.

At that time, and still today, I was concerned because there were some teachings of the Church that I simply could not accept. I had sincere questions and cared about such issues as birth control, which was a hot one at that time and still is. Now many Catholics in the United States and elsewhere in the world just think the Church is wrong about that issue. The marvel to me, is they still seem to be good practicing Catholics. But in 1966 that was all but impossible. And it took a lot of courage for them to defy their Church. At that time, many of us, including experts who were at Vatican II—such as Father Godfrey Diekmann and Father Bernard Haring, the foremost moral theologian of the last century—were hoping and praying that Pope Paul VI would not issue an encyclical on birth control. Father Haring had been a close friend and confidant of the Pope and even preached a private retreat to him. They all told him not address the issue. A widely held suspicion is that the Curia put the pressure on the Pope, telling him he would not be a good Pope if he didn't issue the encyclical. And I think many people think it is going to be one of the worst decisions in the Church's history, clearly showing the crisis of the dictatorial power structure of the Church.

I remember not long before I was ordained a priest hearing some of my mother's longtime friends discussing how their children were coping with controlling the size of their families. One of their marvelous remedies for making sure pregnancy didn't occur was for the wife to make her husband stand in the corner and say Hail Marys enough times to get him out of the mood. This was in the forties. The Church's official solution was the rhythm method, and there are all kinds of kids running around to prove that that method didn't work.

In my speech at the retreat, I said that at that time I would be afraid to talk about birth control with many of the hierarchy (and I still feel the same today). Once when Bishop Carberry was visiting me he said that any couple who had four children had more than done their duty to society and to the Church. *But* he didn't mean they could use any artificial means of birth control. I felt like saying, "Bishop, I sure don't think the rhythm method works. I have families that have six children already and they are not even forty years of age. Are they supposed to live as brother and sister the rest of their lives?" I mentioned this not to find fault with the Church or any particular bishop or cardinal (*in pectore*). For some couples—for many couples—the rhythm method just doesn't work. (Nor does the present-day solution, the so-called Billings method).

I still remember, thank God, a number of older priests who, knowing my zeal and enthusiasm, cautioned me, "Father Fred, take it easy on the birth controllers." And I was naive. When I was in my first parish I asked a monk, Father Ermin, "Why can't they abstain when they're supposed to? Why would they need to do it more than once or twice a month?" (Typical dumb priest remark.)

This seasoned sage said, "Father, you don't sleep with a beautiful woman." Another monk who was later at Vatican II, Father Godfrey Diekmann, told me early on, "Fred, the Church has to do something about this issue."

I thank God that he and others warned me to take it easy on birth controllers. Certainly in earlier times birth control was less of an issue. Many people needed to have large families to work on the farms, help in the trades. And in the past our mortality rates were higher than they are now. But these were not the facts in the 1940s, 1950s, and on. The best minds in the Church have been for a long time concerned about the issue, and yet still nothing has been done. Even today if I were to get up in a pulpit and tell the people, "Do what the doctor tells you on the birth control," I feel sure I would be silenced by the Church hierarchy. It still is not an issue the pulpit can confront, but it is undoubtedly a main concern of Catholic people, and unless you're in the trenches working with these people you have no idea what a struggle it is for very good people. In all my evangelization work through the years the overemphasis on the sin you are committing if you practice birth control has done more harm to drive people from the church than any other issue except perhaps money. And also it is probably the main reason for the decline in confessions. Thank God, the confessional seems to be coming back!

As I said, in the 1960s, 85 percent of the experts from every field—Church lawyers, clergymen, doctors, prominent laypeople—tried to tell the Pope it would be better not to say anything about birth control at that time than to say something negative. The important thing for all of us to remember about this is that Humanae Vitae is not an infallible teaching of the Church.

It was good that I got to at least voice my crises of faith, and despite those crises, my years in Remington/Wolcott were glorious. I finally resolved not to let my doubts lead me away from all the great beliefs of the Church. Vatican II made my years at Sacred Heart one of the most uplifting times of my priesthood. Many of the ideas I had already initiated before Vatican II made it easier for our parish to accept and even to rejoice in the changes. And I hoped Logansport would be as open to the new opportunities the Church was now offering.

9

Light and Darkness

Compared to my other parishes, Logansport's St. Joseph's Church (now All Saints) was huge and the town was more urban. But I was beginning to be much more sure of myself and my abilities. Everything looked as if it would work out. The previous pastor of our Logansport church, although he didn't agree with the Vatican II changes, had practiced Holy Obedience. He had redecorated the church—throwing out the old statues, turning the altar to face the people, replacing the cross of the crucified Christ with a huge beautiful carving of the Glorified Christ. So physically we had a promising beginning, although not one all of the parishioners liked.

One of the most pleasant surprises that I had the first day I arrived at Logansport was finding a nice little Italian girl, Anita Ricci, sitting on my doorstep. She told me the previous pastor had recommended she come and see me for a possible secretarial job. "Glory be to God," I said, "there's nothing I would like better than to have a parish secretary." I had had volunteer secretaries in several parishes, but there is nothing like a paid secretary on the job five days a week. However, it's against my policy to make too many big changes when I first go into a new church, so I told Anita I had to do a little footwork to be sure the parish would accept the position as enthusiastically as I would.

Sure enough, the powers that be said, "You have an elderly retired man already taking care of all of the secretarial needs." My mouth dropped. Then luckily I ran into a man who wielded great influence not only among the Italian people but also throughout the parish. Some seven years later I found they often called him the Pope. After I told him of Anita's offer, he immediately took my side and did the footwork that needed to be done, and I had my first paid secretary. She stayed with me throughout my years in Logansport and was always not only efficient but also pleasant.

Father Dick Weisenberger, the man who became my pastoral associate for several years in Logansport, was not prone to pay people compliments when they were just doing their job, but he paid her a great compliment after he had been in the parish a short time. "You know, Fred," he said, "even more than you and I, people often get their first impression of the parish from the secretary who answers the phone and the doorbell. And thank God Anita's good at it."

If you've ever called a parish to find out when the Masses were scheduled you know how abrupt some answers can be, especially over a Holy Day or holiday. Thank God for patient secretaries, because sometimes after the forty-ninth call a priest or housekeeper can sound almost rude. It isn't good to be abrupt, because you never know who is on the other end of the line. I think of a parishioner by the name of Geneva who used to answer my calls to her home with an abrupt and harsh, "*hello*." Then when she realized who it was, she would change to a melodious tone: "Oh, hello, Father."

When Anita first became my secretary, however, I

didn't really worry about how she was going to receive the parishioners. I was most concerned that she understand the need for confidentiality. "People will pump you for information just as they have my mother, " I told her. And my mother's advice to her was, "You have to be deaf, dumb, and blind." My mother and Anita became great friends. What a way to begin a new pastorate! I had a full-time secretary and a housekeeper who was also my best friend.

My mother had by this time been my housekeeper for many years. The work was light but the position, being the priest's mother, was often more that of a social secretary than housekeeper. The social occasions that my mother arranged were opportunities for her to participate, and with her sharp wit and keen sense of humor she was always a welcome addition to any gathering. Luella, as I indicated in the early chapters, had been bruised by life and wounded by the callousness of her beloved Church. She had been the object lesson by which the Church could keep potentially deviant parishioners in line. Yet, in these later years, she was far from resentful and was exceptionally grateful to have a place, a position of some dignity and even honor in our parish. It is interesting, however, to see what the years do to people, how the automatic submission to authority and the reverence for order affect their behavior.

My mother loved her martini, and unless it was a special occasion, *martini* was singular. She was aging and had experienced all the aches and pains that long life generally blesses us with. The martini in the afternoon was a ritual and a reward for having lived another day. But drinking during the day was seen as a sign of dependence, and no respectable woman wanted to be thought of as having a drinking problem. So the issue was when is it evening and no longer "during the day"? Four o'clock seemed a good compromise, so as the afternoon dragged on, my mother would watch the clock for the slowly moving hand to finally give permission to proclaim the day's work over and reward legitimate. She did have some trouble getting her biological clock in sync with official time when fall brought the change from daylight saving time to regular time. It would be several weeks before she ceased feeling cheated out of an hour. The subservience to order with which we (especially we Catholics?) often live our lives sometimes causes us to make decisions for all the wrong reasons.

With my mother and Anita smoothing the way, everything in this new parish seemed to be going well. But in a very short time that all changed. Since the church was relatively large, it really required two priests in order to run efficiently. That's where problems began. I had not been pastor of a church of this size up to this time, and I had never had an associate before. The bishop called me in and told me of the young man he would like to place with me—a young priest who occasionally had a drinking problem and whose current pastor was anxious to get rid of him.

I was a little apprehensive about having an associate, because I had heard that some of the young priests were no longer as "humble" as most of their predecessors had been in the past. In fact, they could get downright rebellious. One of the most hilarious incidents between pastor and associate I still chuckle over.

A pastor in the diocese had the reputation for being very difficult to get along with and his associate, chafing under his command, pulled a stunt on him that still cracks me up. The pastor bought a new doorbell for the rectory. It did everything, even played the noonday and evening Angelus when you pressed it. The associate, who was clever electrically, fixed the bell so it would no longer play music; in fact it, wouldn't ring at all. The pastor, in a terrible temper, complained vehemently to the merchant who had sold him the expensive toy. The man came to check, and the associate had rewired it so it was working. This was repeated two or three times. The pastor finally angrily returned the nonfunctioning bell!

But the man I was to accept was more openly rebellious than this young priest. He had dared to argue with his pastor, and when they couldn't agree he had sufficient means to buy his own house and had moved out. At this particular time, in the late sixties, moving out of the rectory was unheard of and intolerable.

I was willing to accept this maverick. Knowing his background and the trouble he had already caused, I was concerned whether or not we could get along. I asked him if he thought it was a good idea for us to consult a Purdue psychologist concerning our compatibility. (I knew he already had a degree in professional counseling, unheard of at this time for a priest, so I anticipated his agreement.) We made an appointment and took the test. When we returned for the results of our evaluation, the psychologist first addressed himself to me, saying, "You are a liar. You answer questions to make yourself look good." I was chagrined until he turned to my would-be associate and said, "And *you* really are a liar." We got along fine.

The associate chosen for me demonstrated great creativity. I felt that I could offer him an accepting environment that would cause him to straighten himself out and be productive, but I did not want him living in the rectory or eating there because that would be difficult for my housekeeper (my mother), who was up in years. My request was a definite deviation from the *order* of things.

106

But the bishop was agreed and I now began my years in Logansport with a full-time housekeeper, secretary, and associate, but the string of associates who followed this first young man, Father Pat, were a test of my loyalty to the Church.

Father Pat did everything well. He got along with the youth. I gave him as much free rein as I could. Father Pat was a good musician. As a result, we had the first guitar Mass in the whole diocese except on the college campuses. That was especially exciting to the young adults. My associate was a priest who could relate to the youth and keep them active in the church. With his degree in psychology he was very good at counseling people of all ages. He was good with the sick and the aged. He was excellent in a quality so lacking in so many of us hard-boiled old Church priests: he was very kind and understanding of all human foibles.

During this first year, Father Pat suggested we take an associate friend of his, one who had had considerable trouble, had been disruptive in four or five previous parishes, and needed one more chance. He was not a child abuser or guilty of fiscal misconduct. He was a manic-depressive who tended to enjoy his manic highs so much that he was prone to go off his medication from time to time. Father Pat, with his degree in psychology, told me not to worry. He would take care of him and would let him room with him in his apartment.

Showing no signs of his mental problems, my new associate worked hard with Father Pat for over a year and the parish was blessed and prospered in the areas that he oversaw. With Father Pat he also was a musician with a real flair for contemporary worship. He led young families and teenagers in experiences that were exceptional. However, after a while he worked so hard and such long hours that I felt concern for his health. Yet he only worked harder and harder, longer and longer, and his creativity seemed to, if anything, increase. Unaware of the tendencies of folks with bipolar disorders, I was grateful for an associate who could do so much—the work of three people.

We were able to make many of the changes required by Vatican II. All seemed to be going well. Near the end of my first year in Logansport, however, in June, Father Pat told me he was going to take the next year off. He was bothered by much about the Church. Interested in Jungian psychology, he wanted to go to Zurich, primarily to work through his own personal problems from a Jungian perspective. However, he became so enthralled with his studies he stayed five years and became a certified Jungian analyst. Rather than returning to the United States, he went to Australia to set up his practice. While he did not continue as a priest, in his first years in Australia much of his work was with young priests and nuns.

The bishop was upset by Father Pat's decision. He felt that I couldn't "handle" my associates. The other Catholic clergy in town were sure I couldn't and held me responsible for all the town's youthful revolts. This was 1971.

Then one day around Thanksgiving of that second year, my other associate said he was getting high. After Father Pat had left, I had noticed he, who had been so quiet, so reserved, seemed to be getting hyperactive. I called a psychiatrist. The psychiatrist prescribed medicine, but despite his orders, my associate quit taking his medication. My mother and I tried hiding it in his food, but to no avail.

Crazy things began to happen in January. In one sermon he upset our ardent football fans by suggesting they ought to drop a bomb on the Super Bowl and then he came home to turn the Super Bowl on the TV. He managed to get on President Eisenhower's funeral train to convey his condolences to Mamie on the loss of Ike. One day he disappeared and turned up in Washington at the inauguration of President Nixon. Telling the press he was from St. Joseph's parish in Indiana, dressed as a clown he stood on the Capitol steps exhorting the congressmen to lead Christian lives.

Not long after he returned, I got a call from a merchant in Kokomo saying he'd been skinned. The priest had bought a bunch of merchandise, bats and balls, and had gone about distributing them to kids. His check had bounced. But the merchant was understanding. He said he had a son who was manic-depressive and didn't want to call the police.

I didn't want him getting into the church funds, so I hid all the church checkbooks. I didn't consider worrying about the Mass fund. I knew he wouldn't get into that. He did. But he was charming. The parishioners didn't want to have him arrested. We had a meeting in the parish hall, and in front of the congregation I told him he had to give me all the keys to the church. The parishioners were shocked and angry—at me!—except one man who told them to quiet down, that I was right. Reluctantly, very reluctantly, they agreed.

Father Pat was true to his word that he would be responsible for the priest. He came back from Switzerland and tried to work with him. We all felt he was again under control, taking his medications.

Then he disappeared.

And in two or three weeks I got another call from Kokomo. Another check had bounced from the same merchant. The priest was clever. He carried three different checkbooks, which all looked alike. The merchant had been suspicious, of course, and called the bank in Marian where the check appeared to be from. There were more than sufficient funds there, *but* the check was really on a different bank in which there were no funds.

Now came the real confrontation. The police were called. We searched; they searched. No one could find him. Then suddenly we found he had returned to Logansport in a rental car. His had been impounded. He had visited with several parishioners. One finally called the police.

The police went to her home. My associate was quiet, willing to go with them, only asked if he could please use the bathroom.

The policemen frowned and looked questioningly at the lady of the house. She assured them no six-foot, 220-pound man could possibly get through that little bathroom window. When he didn't come out, the sheriff entered the restroom to note the window open, a window through which he could see the runaway priest making his final getaway.

Finding his car blocked, he took the sheriff's car, which had been left with the keys in the ignition, the motor running. After a pursuit in which he used the police radio in the car to misdirect the chase, he was finally caught and manacled. Eventually he was put in the state hospital, from which he escaped, hopping a freight and disappearing in Chicago. This priest was never removed from his ordination status or even his ministerial duties until he, in a way, removed himself by calling a press conference to announce that he had been married for over a year. As far as I know as of this date, he has for many years now been married to a former nun, who is able to keep him on his medication.

While the wild chase to capture him was going on, I was in my study counseling with a monk from a Franciscan order who had an alcohol problem. My secretary, Anita, would knock on the door and give the latest report on the escapades of the manic-depressive: "The police have cornered him at Mary Lou's."

Forty-five minutes later another knock on the door: "He went out the bathroom window.

Next rap: "He stole the police car."

The monk laughed again and again. "Sounds like the Keystone Cops," he said. After this episode, Father Pat went back to Switzerland to pursue his Jungian psychology and this man, taking a leave from his order, became my next associate.

He needed a place to stay. He was a pious Franciscan priest. He had his parents' home to rest up in—in a different county—only eight or nine miles from our church. He said a beautiful Mass and preached a beautiful homily. The parishioners loved him. Sometimes he would have contact with people who gave him booze or he would party at places and get more to drink than he should have. On one occasion when he had too much to drink, he sideswiped a police car on the road. One of the favorite phrases about priests who have drinking problems is, "Father So and So can drink in *any* given quantity." We used to puzzle about certain times in late afternoon and early evening when he would suddenly change from perfect sobriety to a condition in which he could hardly walk. My mother and my secretary when they would get ready for their four o'clock martini (or five o'clock in case of a time change) began to wonder why the fifth of gin would go down so quickly, so they started to pencilmark the bottle and found that he was consuming about eight ounces at a time. No wonder he would reel about and run into a police car on the way home. Whenever I confronted him, he was in denial or he would joke, "Oh, me and my little caper."

Finally the religious order called him back, and my run of bad luck with associates continued. Another problem priest appeared on the scene. He had left my cousin who was a priest in a nice parish. My cousin later scolded, "Why didn't you call me up? I would have told you he was paranoid." He really couldn't get along with anybody. Although he was an Italian himself, he couldn't even get along with the Italians in the parish. One day after he had been there less than a year, I found a note from him saying: "I can't take this abuse any longer," and he just disappeared.

The next associate was fresh out of the seminary and had no record. He had assisted a priest friend of mine before he was ordained and seemed to be a good zealous priest. He was lionized—people told him how great he was and he believed every bit of it.

This associate had, at the insistence of the bishop, lived in the rectory, a routine that was difficult for my aging mother. When the bishop realized the associate had alienated a large population of our parish, he assigned him to another parish. Less than a year later, I couldn't resist grinning when his new pastor complained about how impossible the young associate was.

After this I had just about had it with associates. I was beginning to wonder if there was something wrong with me. Am I that difficult to get along with? However, there are wonderful young priests out there—many of them. And finally I was assigned a delightfully competent associate who was with me for five years, Father Dick Weisenberger.

These examples of the police chase and its aftermath

and of the troubles I had with my first four associates are more humorous and far less tragic than so many of the stories of priestly misconduct or ineffectiveness that are coming out today. But humorous as they are, they show clearly how the Church, even as it mouths the words "Whole People of God," understands that there are people and then there are people. The clergy are set aside not as a class of servants, as originally intended, but as a privileged group immune from the consequences that ordinary people suffer. I suspect that if there was a maintenance man who looked after the chancery facility who didn't show up, who abused financial privilege, and time and again violated the requirements of his position, that person would be long gone, but not a priest. Once ordained, the priest becomes a part of the privileged class that sees itself as "the Church," and even when its members rail at some of the restrictions imposed by those higher up, they realize the power and privilege they enjoy so fully that they will not risk self to challenge order. And so we still have misfits and miscreants in the clergy—but, thank God, we also have many fine priests like the Father Dick who helped make my next five years (1979–84) there a joy.

As I discovered in my first assignment, there is often a power struggle between the pastor and his associates. In many cases the associate's only right is for a Christian burial, and even that right is conditioned by his good behavior. But there was no rivalry between Father Dick and me. He was very good at everything he did, and I gave him free rein in all areas. He visited the sick. He helped me start the Christ Renews His Parish program. He conducted convert classes for large groups. He taught in the grade school. He had adult instruction classes in the Bible. He was a pioneer in helping Catholics learn to read

113

their Bibles. The participants in his classes said he was very knowledgeable and precise. (Before Vatican II Catholic laymen had been told to keep a Bible in their homes to record births and deaths but *not* to read it. The Church felt the laity weren't well enough informed to understand what they read.)

For all practical purposes Father Dick and I had a copastorate. We believed this was the best way to serve the people. But we didn't publicize this policy because we didn't want to wave a red flag. In the 1970s there was still too much of a mind fix that the associate needed to be a subordinate—very subordinate. Unfortunately for me, however, Father Dick's talents were not hidden under any bushel basket. At that time one of the main emphases of the diocese was on campus ministry. Father Leo Piguet enjoyed a fine reputation at Purdue and had a wonderful way of getting the most talented priests to serve at the university level. He prevailed on the powers that be to let Father Dick Weisenberger come to the university, and I lost a fine associate.

In addition to Father Dick, I had a number of priests friends who were helpful to me throughout my years in Logansport. I was fortunate to have friends within my diocese who had the opportunity to be on the cutting edge, such as campus ministers, in particular Father Leo Piguet, whom I always admired and learned from even though he "stole my associate." And outside my familiar arena I also found encouragement. Father Conley remained a dear friend throughout my ministry. Tom was a pastor of an ethnic, conservative parish in the Chicago area facing the trauma of neighborhood changes occurring in urban areas throughout the country. When he would come down to visit for a few rounds of golf and late-night discussions or when we would share a vacation, I would find he and I were often struggling with the same problems. I kept in close contact with some of the scholars I had met at the continuing educational programs at Notre Dame. Richard O'Brien and Morton Kelsey, for example, provided new insights that spurred me on to deeper reflection and then new experimentation. And fortunately, during all my years at St. Joseph's I still had a close relationship with my Presbyterian friend, Reverend Meyers.

At the same time I left Remington for Logansport, Reverend Meyers moved to a church in Kokomo, a town only thirty miles away. With him and other friends from the Presbyterian Church, I would attend lectures in Chicago. My Presbyterian friend became a regular at many of our diocesan functions, retreats, lectures, and seminars, even being asked to take part in leadership of small groups in some circumstances. I attended Presbytery meetings and the two of us with representatives of our respective parishes joined in serious year-long "Serendipity" groups, a process designed to help people come to grips with the hidden motivations that prompt their decisions and to explore scriptural bases for our beliefs. Of all things, we collaborated on a book titled, *The Possibilities of Spiritual Direction in the New Rite of Reconciliation,* he a Protestant pastor and I a priest, still in good standing. Our congregations benefited in joint educational programs and we became resources for finding material to enhance our local programs. We shared in weddings when it was appropriate and in funerals when requested, including the funeral of my mother. My friend delivered the homily in the funeral Mass for my mother, Luella. With most of the priests in the diocese participating, I offered him the Eucharist in full view. I guess folks felt I was mad in my grief, so no one called me to account for that one.

The town of Logansport did not afford the same stimulation toward ecumenical support for my efforts at innovation as Remington. In fact, my ecumenical efforts were to a large extent the causes of much of the hostility some other Catholic clergy felt toward me. The pastors of the two other churches did not want any kind of innovation, Vatican II or otherwise. After one year they arranged with the bishop and personnel board to get me out of town. Fortunately, for once the Church law was on my side. They had a little bit more to reckon with than they expected, because I stayed for thirteen more years and outlasted both of them. The three parishes got consolidated into one. When I came there were seven priests, and there were only two when I left.

But because of my previous experience with my Presbyterian friend, I was able to introduce and make effective a much-talked-about but not-yet-realized collegiality among denominations. I started an ecumenical group, the Ministerial Association, that included many Methodist churches, a Baptist church, a Christian church, a Lutheran church, an Episcopal church, and others. They provided a different kind of personal relationship that enhanced the lives of all of our churches. One of the highlights of our association was an ecumenical celebration of the feast of St. Francis of Assisi in the Episcopal church. The church was packed; the singing was thunderous and beautiful.

It was Reverend Meyers who especially helped me during this period with ideas for forming a parish pastoral council, a concept endorsed by Vatican II but in my part of Indiana only beginning to be seriously considered. One of the best things that I ever did was enter into some serious discussions with my friend concerning the Presbyterian system of local church government. I am Catholic and had no intention of looking for anything that would not fit within our framework. But the Presbyterian church and many of our other Protestant counterparts have practical experience in developing lay leadership in congregational government.

I thought the idea of a parish council would thrill my parishioners, but it is amazing how hard it is to give power away. With power goes responsibility, and laypeople are very comfortable with the understanding that the priest has divine instructions about church decisions and therefore must bear all the responsibility for the results of those decisions. In the eyes of laypeople, Catholics reared in the old Church, to stand before God with a sense of responsibility for a failed program of a costly effort that has not borne fruit is terrifying. Better to rubber-stamp what says than to come up with ideas for which they might be responsible.

But with the knowledge from my Protestant friends as to how to make parish councils work, St. Joseph's began exploring new ways to train lay leaders, new understandings of the interpersonal dynamics in groups, new ways to validate people in their decisions and to put the focus on process as well as results. We developed a strong parish council. It is well that we had that preparation. During my tenure there, we faced one of the most controversial decisions that a Catholic parish encounters: how to go about closing a long-standing parochial school operating with a deficit, consolidating it with the other Catholic school in town, and assigning the pupils of the consolidation to two already-existing school buildings.

For folks with three generations of children reared in the same church and educated at the same school any kind of consolidation is so unwelcome it stirs up animosity. So many of our parishes throughout the country face the same circumstance. It costs more and more to educate children in a parochial setting, and fewer and fewer families are committed to the cost of sustaining such an education. Yet the school is tradition. And the diocese decided to consolidate into one grade school but to keep two grade school buildings open in Logansport. Our school at St. Joseph's (now All Saints) was to remain open. The school at St. Bridgit's had been closed for some time, but the building was still in good condition, while St. Vincent's school building was a shambles. So St. Vincent's students were to be reassigned, some to St. Bridgit's and others to St. Joseph's. And I was the priest who with our parish council had to see to the consolidation.

Even though I did not always agree with the decisions our parish council made concerning the means to facilitate consolidation, I was incredibly proud of the manner in which the lay leadership went about making decisions. They gathered data, looked at alternatives, faced all possibilities, and, above all, were willing to bear the responsibility for their decisions. That effective parish council was one very good result of Vatican II.

Working with the parish council and other lay committees is one way for a priest to come to know his congregation better. But another is certainly secular social events. One of our most anticipated parties was the Spitznoggle family's annual hog roast. The family invited the whole congregation. We even celebrated Mass at the event. As a priest I've learned that while some people who need help will seek me out at church, others are more comfortable sharing their problems with me indirectly at such functions as a hog roast. What begins there often continues in the confessional or in private conferences. This Spitznoggle hog roast paved the way for other parties in a popular meeting place on the Tippicanoe river. Since I don't drink, I can remember a number of occasions when my conversations at these parties turned into consultations.

Does it sound like my later years at St. Joseph's, now All Saints, were all fun and games? Not so. A parish is never without problems. At the beginning of the last year there—trouble! Since the school's population had increased, I had negotiated with the Motherhouse for several new nuns to teach at our expanded grade school. I had planned for them to live at St. Bridget's rectory. But my new associate spoiled that plan by just moving into that rectory. Now, there was no place for them. However, living alone, I really didn't need the wonderful large rectory I had been in since coming to Logansport, so I moved across the street to a smaller house. When St. Joseph's school had been smaller it had been the convent for the nuns who taught there. The new nuns were happy to be in a roomy house so near the grade school. And I was delighted with my smaller quarters. Problem solved.

Later we had an even more difficult problem than the consolidation of schools. In 1983, the diocese had a new progressive bishop from the East, Bishop George A. Fulcher. We had seven priests in Logansport and three churches. In part because of the increasing shortage of priests, but mainly because of the duplication of efforts. Bishop Fulcher decided one church was enough. Logansport is a railroad town, which had a much larger population when the railroads were a prime means of transportation. Its parishes all stemmed from those early days and were in the beginning oriented according to nationality. St. Vincent's parishioners were all Italian, St.

Joseph's German, and St. Bridgit's Irish. But such divisions had long ceased to be relevant. It had been ages since people had chosen their church because of the nationality of its congregation. Bishop Fulcher saw little need for three churches within a mile of one another. I was pastor of St. Joseph's. Eight blocks to the west was St. Bridget's and eight blocks to the east St. Vincent's. Each church had its own parochial school building, although St. Bridgit's and St. Vincent's hadn't had students for a number of years.

The bishop made plans to consolidate the three churches into one—St. Joseph's, to be renamed All Saints. When Bishop Fulcher was killed in an auto accident in January of 1984, his close friend and confidant Charles Kline urged the new bishop, William L. Higi, to go through with the consolidation. So Kline and Father Fred turned the three parishes into one, St. Joseph's, which became All Saints. To say that some of the parishioners of St. Bridgit's and St. Vincent's were unhappy is an understatement. Even St. Joseph's people were unhappy because those "other people" were taking their seats.

The consolidation over, I was pleased when the bishop assured me that Logansport would be my residence for the rest of my life.

That was January of 1985. In April I was told I had to leave town. I'm sure the powers that be decided a new face could better deal with the unrest among the displaced laity. And I suppose I still thought that as a pioneer initiating this change I ought to have some say in the matter. I certainly felt capable of handling the new consolidated parish.

I had been reluctant to leave parishes in the past. One always feels he is leaving his children behind. I had never felt, however, that a move was punitive. For the first time, however, I did with this move. It was a very painful time for me. When I left Logansport for my current position in semiretirement, I left an adventure that will never be finished because of my age.

All in all, during those years at Remington and Logansport I had the opportunity to try new things, to test the teasing possibilities of Vatican II, to see what it might mean to structure my ministry, not after a blind obedience to order, the way it had always been done and the way those who had always done it wanted it done, but after a vision of Christ's compassion for the world and the example of skilled practitioners of the art of ministry. I did not change the world, but I did present new possibilities to folks so they could see the alternatives and choose for themselves what was good. I did help laypeople taste the satisfying experience of an active and vital part in our mission. I did help introduce ways to educate our young for a future in which they can think for themselves even as they live for their Lord. We always bemoan the fact that there are never enough priests. The problems that this raises are relieved when we have a virtual army of millions of equipped Christians to share leadership, to encourage, to support the priests we do have. I hope I left a message for those who will hear in a cynical world filled with excuses and rationalization the distant invitation to joy.

10

Are the Shades Being Drawn?

My move to Carmel opened up new possibilities in my apostolate. First, however, I had to get over the hurt of supposedly being demoted and betrayed. I was still a priest in Logansport when I was summoned to appear before the personnel board and the bishop at a two-hour meeting. Ten minutes into the meeting I put down on the outline of the agenda of the meeting three words: "Fred is Out." And I felt a panic inside. I didn't know where I was going. The bishop, who had told me in January that I could stay in Logansport the rest of my life, said it was absolutely necessary that I leave Logansport and take a different assignment. I had been a pastor for thirty-six years, and I couldn't believe that I was going to have to consider a new post, possibly even outside the diocese. An hour and a half into the meeting, I looked across the table at him and said, "Bishop, if you are about to tell me that I have to go back to a little country parish, I am *not* going." I knew I was too old to take on cheerfully or successfully the role I had once loved of being priest of a small parish—I could no longer be chaperone for high school youth, janitor, bookkeeper, liturgist, choir director. I couldn't go to every diocesan meeting, shovel the snow, and maybe sweep the classrooms in addition to my roles as homilist, and confessor. I felt I was too old to do a good job in a small parish.

He said, "Fred, don't back me into a corner."

I looked him right in the eye across the table and said, "Bishop, we are *in* that corner." The bishop had to go for fresh air and I followed him out and embraced him, saying, "I don't want to be contrary, but I cannot do what you have in mind. I'm sorry."

Without realizing it, I had really stirred up a hornets' nest. The meeting had already been too long so it was adjourned without anything being settled.

Shortly after this, the bishop had a meeting with diocesan consultants. I became their chief agenda. Father Dick was a diocesan consultant, so when the bishop proposed, "Fred's just bluffing. Send him a letter and he will go," Father Dick, in his emphatic crystal-clear way, pounded the table and declared, *"Fred is not bluffing."* He knew me. He had to repeat the message several times before they got it. They all left the meeting wondering what to do with me.

The evening after their meeting I was home with a terrific headache. I wondered if I could at sixty-seven contact another diocese or some holy sister at some convent that needed a chaplain. About eight-thirty I was ready for bed when I remembered what an Irish monsignor had told me in my earlier days in the priesthood—when he really needed to sleep, he disconnected the telephone and said, " I need my sleep. The whole damned universe can go to hell."

However, I did not pull the plug. Thank God. I wasn't in bed five minutes, at most ten, when the phone rang and I answered it. It was the bishop. He said, "Father Leo Piguet needs help and he said, 'If Fred's available I want him.' "

Then the bishop added, "But I still want you to go to. . . ." and he mentioned the place (a small parish), and I said to him, "Bishop, I wouldn't go there for all the tea in China." In deference to the bishop years later, I can see that his wanting to put me in that small parish was complimenting me, because it was a trouble spot where he felt I could probably bring peace and reconciliation. But I was too old. This is not to say had I accepted I would be dead or retired now, but who knows for sure? I was relieved to know I was off the hook and slept soundly, calling and contacting Father Leo within a day or two. We worked out the details.

Unwittingly and certainly against my will and the will of the bishop Father Leo's taking a chance on me has set a precedent in the diocese. I was the first senior associate in the diocese. After my appointment other priests my age have been appointed to serve in that capacity, giving them a chance to function rather than fade into oblivion. So my obstinacy has been a boon to others. And certainly my acting as an associate has given me the chance to exercise more than usual a talent I've had in door-to-door evangelization. But the change was exceedingly difficult for me.

Now suddenly in coming to Carmel I felt in some ways I was back in 1942, in the first three years of my ordination. I saw myself once again as an assistant under orders; do only what you are told to do. It is still the order of the day for associates, assistants, staff, committees to say amen to whatever the pastor wants.

And Father Leo was typical of most pastors. He was a great administrator and a great pastor, but he operated as a one-man team. He ran the whole show. One of the things that was especially hard for me to take was that during the celebration of Holy Week and Easter I had absolutely nothing to do because the pastor did it all. My only function during the Easter vigil was to say a few words after the pastor baptized a number of people.

I would not have survived my last year or so in Logansport or my first years at St. Elizabeth Seton without spiritual direction from my friend Father Morton Kelsey. He had to beat me down to size constantly when I came to Seton: "Fred, you are now a senior associate. You are not a pastor. You have nothing to say. Just be yourself." I wondered if I could continue to function as a priest. I thought, *I don't need to work. I should retire.* I now appreciate Father Andrew Greeley's definition of an associate: "An associate is a mouse on his way to becoming a rat." It took me a long while to give up being the "rat" in charge. My problems were not with the congregation but with issues affecting their right to have a say in the running of their church. I had to be content with just being a mouse.

When I first came to Carmel, St Elizabeth Seton had not yet been built. The congregation was meeting in a local grade school. Jokingly we called ourselves St. Woodbrook after the name of the school. When I first became acquainted with the plans for Seton not a brick had been laid. I was concerned that the proposed $8 million church would not serve the community well even if they could afford it. A church needs to have room to serve the whole congregation's needs. Still today at St. Elizabeth Seton, the people do not have good facilities for religious education, which is most important. Until the church was built, the children received their religious instructions in the homes. It came as quite a shock to the pastor and the staff that after the church was built the parents protested, "You mean that we have spent all this money to build a church and we still have to have religious instruction in the homes?" So we began religious instruction in the church, but as a result of our lack of rooms for the youngsters, Sunday mornings have been a zoo. Classes have had to take place all over the building. Now we have finally finished the church. But does that mean we have rooms for classes in religious education? No. We have fine offices, but we have purchased Quonset huts for our children's classes. And we are in the situation where we have so large a debt we cannot afford to build a Sunday school, let alone an elementary school, which is badly needed in the area. The new pastor has a school very high on his priority, as do most of the parishioners. But we have to face reality. Thanks be to God our current bishop and the financial councils in the diocese will not let a congregation even think about building a school unless they have $3 million.

Having no part in the decision on what type of building would best suit the congregation of St. Elizabeth Seton was the beginning of my having a difficult time learning where I, the senior associate, fit in this parish's administration. During my fourteen years in Logansport, no matter what kind of associate I had, I tried to share with him pastoral responsibility and power. And I tried to share responsibility with the laity. In many cases the people have nothing to say about how the money is gathered and spent—or the administration of the church after it is built. Even though the supposed staff meetings, parish council meetings, pretend to try to convince the people that they are really running the church, most of the time their vote is a simple yes or "amen, whatever you want, Father." Many pastors, including myself, have suffered under the delusion, especially since Vatican II, that we give the people say in all that matters in the parish spiritually, financially, and socially. But as Reverend Craig

Meyers pointed out to me while I was still a pastor, "Fred, in your enthusiasm over Vatican II, you can't claim to give the people a share in the decision making as long as they agree with you but overrule them asserting your pastoral authority as soon as there is disagreement." As a consequence of Craig's just criticism, I have honestly tried to let people have their way even when it was contrary to what I have thought. I believe this is part of the Vatican II directive to have the whole congregation—newly formed parish councils and pastoral associates—included in decision making.

Although after my first years at Seton I have found my niche and have had some of my happiest years as a priest, I have not ceased to be troubled by some of the other mechanics of church administration. In the previous chapter, I mentioned that the most difficult period of my life was in Logansport suggesting and accomplishing the union of three parishes into one. However, I retract that statement. In 1997 Father Leo, God bless him, was ill and wanted and needed to retire, and it would have been good for his health if he could have retired in '97. But the wheels of change creaked slowly along.

I, with the staff and the whole congregation, was most concerned about who would succeed Father Leo. But I had no idea and certainly no input into whom the bishop was considering. A most difficult period in my entire life was from that February to July of '98, when the appointments were settled. Many changes were scheduled for July, although we knew those changes were coming already in February. Probably it is not my concern, but I was very angry because the whole diocese was in the state of limbo for those months. Pastors who know they are going to be changed come July 1 are not about to carry on much of a ministry in those last few months. Why is July

1 the only time you can make changes? When we had a number of new priests it would have made much more sense. Had I been an insider instead of an outsider, a role that I have been accustomed to wear for the last decade or so, it probably would not have bothered me so much. I would have known that the new pastor who was coming was one of the most talented and gifted, a real leader in pastoral and diocesan affairs and very intimate and close friend of my friend Fr. Dick Weisenberger. In fact, some months into his pastorate, I had been quite ill and was concelebrating with him the Mass. At the close I asked him if I could say just a word or two to the congregation. I don't think he was thrilled to let me—but he did. I told the parishioners, "I've been a priest for fifty-eight years and this is one of the most moving celebrations of the Mass I've ever experienced." They applauded Father Ted Rothrock and the music people.

I still have some negative feelings about being a senior associate, but I've come to find that position has been one of the greatest blessings in my life and maybe one of the reasons I am alive today able to function as a priest, to pastor to the people without the administrative headaches of a pastor. It took me a while to realize Father Leo was probably absolutely right. Administration has never been my cup of tea. It is a wonder the parishes have survived in spite of me.

My first duties at Seton were to go out and bless homes, and while this is worthwhile, I felt diminished. Yet it gradually became clear to me that I was needed for that duty and to say Mass, to preach, and to instruct. These were the areas in which I excelled. Between the lines you can probably say I was acting like a kid that's been hurt—a spoiled brat of a kid, a bit rebellious. After all, the reason I'm an associate is because I bucked authority.

One of the main reasons I write the story of my life is because I think more and more that the young man least likely to succeed would not have succeeded without spiritual direction. My spiritual director during my early days at Seton had to raise hell with me over and over again, to tell me, "Fred, you are a senior associate. You chose it. You aren't in charge." I remember Father Damasus Winzen telling me to "let the virtue of humility be the foundation stone of your apostolate! Don't even talk about it in your own soul! With the help of prayer and counseling, the demons will never find a place to stand but drop straight through to hell."

Another spiritual director used to harp at me, "Get in touch with your inner self, know who you are, understand your need for God, and people will come to you. You do far more by what you are than by what you say." Today, more than ever, I respond with, "Amen, Amen, Alleluia."

I think if there is anything we need to realize today, it is that no matter how learned we are, how good our words are, how excellent and polished our homilies might appear to be, what and who we are is the real message. I take great consolation in this particular advice because although I think I'm a good homilist now, I can guarantee you I have been anything but, as Craig pointed out to me years ago. People accepted my advice because of my genuine concern for them, *not* because my sermons moved them. Why didn't somebody tell me how bad I was? Typically, in the Catholic tradition who's going to tell you? Laypeople don't usually comment on the priest's homilies—except to lie and tell him how inspiring he is. The first time I listened to a recording of one of my homilies I almost quit preaching. My only consolation is if you've never heard your voice recording, you never know how bad you sound.

I have found that when I am happy within and I feel as if I am right with God, it helps me to be right with my fellowman—that does not mean that I'm always happy and attractive to people. I resented it when an undertaker once told me, "Father, you're a real professional," as if I really didn't care except for a paycheck.

I'm happy, however, being a senior associate, and I've found that I am, after all, a pioneer in this area. A number of priests have followed my example. Rather than going to a small one-man parish as has been the custom for those of us nearing retirement, many have chosen to become senior associates. I've been congratulated for pioneering again. But in reality I didn't do anything at all. The Lord did it. In this instance, I'm at Seton because there was no other alternative, just as early in my life I wound up in the seminary because there was no place else to go.

And in some ways I have not been stopped from being innovative—not really. Soon after I came to Carmel, I began to walk through the neighborhoods evangelizing. In the beginning, my evangelization came about probably because of my necessity to have something to do. I feel like I'm sure Jesus must have felt at times. He couldn't do much in the synagogue or the ecclesiastical structure of his time, so he traipsed up and down the highways and the byways ministering to the real needs of the people. Any cursory reading of the New Testament would soon tell you that his was a bizarre or at least unusual behavior in freeing people.

God has opened up a chance for me for a ministry I rejoice in, where all of my talents are really put to the test. When I first came to town and went out blessing homes, I was in awe of these "city" people. It wasn't long before I discovered that people are people wherever you go. Nothing has helped me to identify more with Jesus than, in one of the largest growth areas in the state, making cold calls on doors. It's been the biggest challenge of my life, but I like to feel the most productive.

My talents have been put to the test and I like to think I have stood the test and passed. What talents? I guess the ability to talk to and more important *listen* to strangers. Most priests ask me why I make such a fuss over evangelizing. Lord knows I've tried to take priests with me to show them, but they could hardly wait to get back home. Yet at the same time, they've agreed with me that part of our ministry training should be in learning to go out and knock on doors. It is good for priests to find out what's going on in the real world outside our splendid isolated castles and churches.

Why do I say this? Let me give you a few examples. It's no secret that there are many people today who are angry with the Church—particularly the young people. When at different times and places people have told me they are angry with the Church, I have extended my hand and said, "Shake; so am I." And I'm not lying or putting up a false front. Wasn't our Lord angry with established church in his time? When I confess I'm angry, too, part of the value of my ability as a spiritual director comes through, for it often develops that it isn't only the Church the people are angry with but also other problems in their lives. As we talk, they can express their anger and the healing process can begin. Anger itself isn't a sin. It's what you do with it. And excuse me for being preachy, but if there's any one thing we need to be more concerned about it is the violence that erupts on every level—domestic, civil, church, family, state, nation. To be a successful evangelizer and spiritual director, the priest has to first deal with his own anger (angers), which isn't easy. After admitting he is angry with the Church, as these people are, the priest can start applying the medicine of in-depth spirituality. He can help people to face the real challenges of God instead of living only in fear. He can help them to recognize that Jesus as a man was angry and, rather than give up on us, God accomplished our redemption through Him. I am not trying to write a theological treatise on anger but just trying to point up the need for us to recognize our anger even with God. People ask, "How can a good God permit so and so?" Well, he didn't. He gave us free will. To envision God as a punitive, unmerciful monster in the sky is unconscionable. He is the loving father who gave us his son, who was submissive even to death on the cross. Jesus did not come into the world, strange as it might sound, just to act in such a way that he would get crucified. As a good Jew, he had no desire to die at the age thirty-three. He wanted to live and he wants us to live.

In any case, although it sounds like it, I don't preach a homily when I'm evangelizing. But I do try to drop the seeds that might bring somebody who has given up on God eventually—one, two, five years later—back to church.

Not long ago, somebody probably brought up in the old Church of fear, temptation, and damnation knelt behind the screen in a confessional instead of talking to me face-to-face. Almost angrily he said to me, "Father, the only reason I'm kneeling at your side tonight is because you knocked on my door three years ago." To this day I cannot possibly tell you who this person was because he came to me behind the screen.

What do you do when you run into a person who says he has no belief at all? One person who was with me evangelizing was shocked to see me stand and let an angry man proclaim to us and surely half the neighborhood that he was an atheist. I didn't question his right to be an atheist. I simply listened to some of his anger. When it came time to leave, I said my, "God bless you, my dear man," and added, "Oh, excuse me," acknowledging that he doesn't believe that God exists. As we left and went on down the street, my fellow evangelizer rebuked me for not proving to the man that there is a God. And I said to her, "He's no atheist. He is just a man who is madder than hell at God."

I could give many more examples. One of the big fears of most people who consider evangelization is that people will get very angry with you for even daring to knock on their doors. In all the years that I have been doing this, since I first began in 1945 in what had been a Ku Klux Klan area, I think I could count on the fingers of one hand the number of times that people have slammed the door in my face or count on the fingers of my other hand when they were either very abrupt or highly critical and abrasive. I can think of one example. A woman in a very elegant house bitterly recited a litany of negative emotions about religion, about the Church, so I just listened (that is the thing that people have to do—people, particularly priests, have to learn how to listen not preach), and after quite a discussion and as I was ready to go down to the road her husband came home and we had then a much more wonderful joyful discussion.

I might say here what has been a source of anger to me is that sometimes after I have encouraged people to come back to Church, when and if they do, they find the Church now is like the Church they left. What they didn't like about it hasn't changed. And speaking of that, one of the most common complaints I've met through all the years is that all priests, preachers, councilmen of the Church want is money.

I might say with a certain amount of pride that a councilman once told me, "Father, that is the best money talk I've heard you give in the six years you've been here thus far." Then after a short pause he said, "Come to think of it, that's the only money talk I've heard you give in six years." In Logansport, Father Dick and I felt if we did our job well, the people would come through. And they did.

I feel now that these last fifteen years of my ministry have been among the happiest of my life. I am allowed to work in a marvelous parish in Carmel, Indiana, a very affluent suburb of Indianapolis. I have access to all the advantages that both city and suburb provided for me at a time in life when I am relieved of the full responsibility for a parish and its administration. I work with a fine staff and am fully appreciated by a wonderful congregation. I no longer feel burdened by the onus of being "least likely." I have long since come to terms with my limitations and my capabilities and have felt a power in preaching, a confidence that I never quite possessed in my former parishes. But I also have been more frustrated than at virtually any other time in my life. While I feel comfortable with myself, I sometimes feel more alienated from my Church than anytime in the past. Yet a priest does not exist except in intimate relationship with the Church he serves or at least the Church through which he serves Christ.

During my later years in Logansport and the first years in Carmel, the results of the sixties more and more put in question our moral and ethical values. Is it any wonder that the Church felt justified by society and vindicated in the new direction our history took in returning to the ways of the past? The tendency to return to the old order has been reflected in the Church that has felt vindicated by what we see in society.

The current Pope, while none can doubt his sincerity and his courage as a product of World War II, has espoused the absolutism and the unquestioned authority that have kept the Church's greatest gifts, its people, all its people, well aware of the place they occupy and the only place they can occupy in the Church's structures. The hope of men gifted in ordained ministry also being able to have families has been eliminated even as a topic of conversation. The old apologetic of honoring women but not really respecting their gifts for ministry is once more in vogue. The invitation for all to come to the table with equal respect but different gifts has become an order to get back in line and keep quiet.

It is sad to me that at this point of my most satisfying ministry I am seeing the Church's ability to reach its potential in service to a world at the point of its greatest need. From Carmel, Indiana, I am a man under orders but increasingly hesitant to be a part of the order as a submissive supporter of the status quo. I cannot do much now to bring about change. But who cares if an eighty-year-old priest is eccentric? I hope that some reader of this book might.

11

Reflections near Journey's End

One of the advantages, and at the same time one of the afflictions, of living a long time is the inevitable need to make some sense out of life. Looking back over the past eighty-plus years, even as I look around me at the world of 2000, I sometimes feel like the preacher Ecclesiasticus: "Vanity of vanities. . . ." The need to question, the elusiveness of answers, the meaning of life, and the desperate need to feel that my part in it makes sense all swirl around in the head of one who has been an arbiter of faith for almost sixty years. A priest, semiretired (whatever that means), still proclaiming the Word and still administering the sacraments, grateful to be active but needing to know if all that activity makes one bit of difference in the long run, I find myself asking all the eternally recycled questions about the meaning of life.

What is the Church, at its spiritual best, at its practical worst, and as an ultimate reality? Six decades after ordination, those are questions that trouble an eighty-year-old priest. Those are questions that cut to the heart of my identity. Those are questions that accompany me to my ultimate encounter with my God. As a man, judged by so many of my earliest authorities, as the youngster "least likely to succeed," now I am surrounded by years of vocational loyalty and functional accomplishment which ought to entitle me to the ecclesiastical equivalent of a gold watch and a confident expectation of that, "Well done, good and faithful servant," we all hope for at our passing.

Though I have never climbed the structural level of success beyond local parishes, I think I have good friends and testimonials to comfort me in these later years. But the haunting question keeps recurring as I shed with some satisfaction the label as one "least likely." What is success? At the heart of this query is the need to know what the Church ought to be, what a Christian ought to be, and who I am in light of what I have done. Have I been the faithful disciple or merely a blindly devoted functionary carrying out the will of equally blind functionaries who have more authority? Is the Church the bearer of God's hope for humankind or a caricature that inhibits the completion of the Lord's real work of reconciling all humanity to himself and one another? Can we dismiss the failures of the Church as incidental in the light of greater accomplishments? Or, as sinful human beings, must we all bear the scrutiny of our Lord's standards while trembling before the possibilities we might uncover?

What changes are needed for the Church to carry on God's work? This is the crucial question, crucial for the next infant baptized in the arms of believing parents, crucial to the bright-eyed children receiving first communion. It is crucial to the eager newly ordained and should be crucial to the bishop wielding power. It is crucial to me in the evening of my work. No matter what others say, this is the frightening question that prompted this book.

In his poem "The Mending Wall" Robert Frost states, "Good fences make good neighbors." Though his poem questions this contention, there is something about separation that keeps things in their intended arrangement. Strong walls make for good order. For those in the Catholic Church who love order, good walls are the first essential. But for those of us who feel we have to break through the walls from time to time, Vatican II has opened some cracks and has rattled the foundations enough that other fissures are possible.

Everyone who remembers the shock of some of the changes within the Church during those years in the late sixties has a different perspective on what was most important, what caused the most radical changes. Certain things, however, stand out as direct results of Vatican II:

One is the recognition of the premise that the Church is the whole Church, clergy and laity. That was made manifest when the Mass began to be celebrated in native languages. It was important that the laity with all their experience from the secular world understand the words and, therefore, the meaning of the Holy Eucharist.

Another result was that it became more important that our homilies are relevant.

New music was created to express the liberation of joy within the worshiping community.

Liturgical experimentation began that strove to include all the people in the liturgical experience.

The appearance of nuns educated in so many of the more technical skills of social service and, heaven help us, out of uniform began to shake traditional views of the religious and their function.

Churches began to develop lay leadership with real authority as parish pastoral councils were formed. The hope that the pastor could spend time doing that for which he was trained instead of being lost in administrivia was becoming a real possibility.

The sacrament of Penance became more than ritual

and could be, if used fully, an opportunity for spiritual direction, an instrument for transformation of behavior and personality.

In short, the impulses begun by Vatican II have been creating cracks to allow holy change in the Church. Many see these changes as renewal, but others see only catastrophic disorder. Even as I write this in 2000, it is evident that the hierarchy of the Church is still very reluctant to empower the people as Vatican II outlined. Characterized as battles between old guard and new guard, conservative and liberal, discipline and permissiveness, obedience and rebellion, the birthing of tomorrow's Church can be read in this struggle.

Some of the main struggles that have surfaced since Vatican II are those that concern (1.) the new approaches to the Rite of Penance; (2.) the role of women in the Church; (3.) the sharing of communion with those of other faiths; (4.) the rules relating to marriage; (5.) the birth control issue. All of these issues became dominant in my final two parishes in Logansport and Carmel, so I would like to touch on them briefly here.

The new *Rite of Penance* opened the way for confession to be an opportunity for spiritual direction, a more positive influence in the lives of both priests and parishioners. Indirectly, Vatican II has shown us how important spiritual direction is for all of us, clergy and laity. We priests need to recognize the dark sides, the shadow sides of our personalities and deal with them. The best way for us to be good shepherds is for us to love ourselves, to recognize our insufficiencies and deal with them so that we can be not only more sincere but also much more effective in dealing with the people who come to us. This is what good spiritual directors such as Father Damasus Winzen and Father Godfrey Diekmann enable us to do, and I hope

139

more and more of our priests will become proficient in this area. Spiritual direction can open up whole new worlds for the priest and enable him to share those worlds with those under his care and help them expand their worlds. The priest and his parishioners grow together as the whole people of God. Unless a priest recognizes the fact that he needs spiritual direction, he will never seek it. If a priest doesn't have spiritual direction himself, how can he give it to others? *Nemo dat quod nun habet.* No one can give to others what he does not have.

Women's roles are slowly changing. The nuns are indeed freer. They can choose to be in or out of habit, to be much more closely involved in the lay world. Laywomen, too, have a much more important role in their parishes, but the position of women still has a long way to go. We are all familiar with what many of the women want and their struggles to have their voices heard in the Church, because the newspapers lay and religious have been full of these problems.

The same cannot be said about the concerns relating to *communion* or *marriage,* but these issues are equally pressing. Most parishes still follow the rule most of us know, which is that only the faithful in good standing can receive communion. No communion is to show unity or mutual recognition with other traditions. Yet the canon law of the Church says communion can be shared with people of other faiths under certain conditions. I was so happy to discover this canon in the code of canon law. It makes so much sense to me and to many other priests who want to minister to the people and believe that salvation is for all. Tough as it is on pioneers, nothing would ever change unless they did it. And from time to time some pioneer priests have followed the canon law on communion even though the bishops have chosen to ignore and even reject that particular canon. Parenthetically, many people are puzzled that Christ's words from the Last Supper, "Take this, *all* of you, and eat it for this is my body which is given up for you," refers only to Catholics in good standing.

To illustrate, in the late fifties I presided at the wedding of a doctor's daughter who was marrying a non-Catholic in a parish other than mine. She was very distraught by the idea of her husband not being able to receive communion with her during their sacrament. She said, " I want to be united with this man for life in holy marriage. Why can't we be united at the Lord's table, becoming one in Christ just as we do in matrimony?" I knew the pastor would not accept the groom receiving the host. There was no point in telling this pastor it was within canon law. So I solved the problem, albeit surreptitiously. I gave the bride two wafers so she could share with her bridegroom at this, the first Mass of their lives together. Amen. And not long after that her husband became Catholic.

The harm that this rule, which really isn't a valid rule, has done to Catholics marrying non-Catholics can hardly be imagined. One of the things I have found out from evangelization, especially from door-to-door cold calls, is that nothing has caused more people to leave the Church than this kind of attitude, enforced so strongly up to the present time.

In relation to marriage, there were and are still several rules that often infuriate or confuse both Catholics and non-Catholics. One forbids the priest to preside at a marriage during Lent. In the late sixties, I knew a priest who was a pacesetter like myself. Serving in a parish on a college campus, he was trying to follow the rules of the Church but also trying to do what a couple wanted for

141

their marriage. He diplomatically got over the Church's objection to the couple being married on Palm Sunday, which they wished, by suggesting to them it would be cheaper to use Easter Sunday's flowers for the service. But maverick that he was, although this was before Vatican II, he did not insist that the bride agree to raise the children Catholic and he offered to include whatever portions of her Episcopal rite she wished in the marriage service.

To allow Episcopal words in a Catholic rite! Unthinkable! Worship in churches other than Catholic for many years was only allowed with permission. The language of the Church is exclusively designed to keep the faithful in; even the title *Church* is intended to describe "the Church." Doctrinal truth is described and proscribed by the Church, and it is clear that the Church has sole possession of the keys to the kingdom, both here and hereafter, and the control of who can share in the sacraments of grace has been seen as tantamount to the power to bestow or withhold salvation. Granted there have been some changes in the rules since Vatican II. Now non-Catholics marrying Catholics no longer must sign a paper agreeing to raise their children Catholic. While the Church hopes the children will be raised Catholic, this no longer has to be down on paper.

But again in relation to marriages, they are sanctioned or forbidden on the basis of canon law that is forbidding in its complexity, tortuously difficult for the uninitiated, but manipulated with relative ease for the powerful. The walls within which order has traditionally been maintained with rigidity and absolute authority have been high indeed. In the late forties a friend of mine who wanted to be married to a Catholic had had a completely justifiable divorce and needed an annulment. He was told it might be nine years before that could occur and he could wed in the church. Annulment is still an issue.

Another issue related to marriage that has plagued the Church for years and is still unresolved is *birth control*. This has not been solved by Vatican II, but because of Vatican II, some of the laity no longer anguish over the Church's rules in these cases.

A monk who was later at Vatican II, Father Godfrey Diekmann, told me early on, "Fred, the Church has to do something about this issue." The best minds in the Church have been for a long time concerned about the issue, and yet still nothing has been done. It still is not an issue the pulpit can confront, but it is undoubtedly a main concern of Catholic people, and unless you're in the trenches working with these people you have no idea what a struggle it is for very good people.

The Church, with all its divine nature, is also an institution living within and affected by the world in which it exists. The power of the Church in the past was great because its parishioners were largely uneducated people. When I was first ordained a priest, I was often the only college-educated man in the community. Now that's no longer the case. And just like many priests I am not alone in thinking the Church has to come to grips with an entirely different lifestyle and has to rub elbows with the educated and learn to consider their choices rather than being obedient to absolutes. The Church cannot erect walls high enough to keep out all alien ideas, and the most alien idea of all to the Church is that each individual has the capacities and the rights to think for himself.

Pope John Paul II feels this "alien idea" is especially true in the United States. He calls us cafeteria Catholics. One of the recent Popes, however, stated, "The primacy of

143

one's conscience is above all law." But it is true that conscience has to be well informed and mature. And that still remains a primary function of the Church. Thank God we cafeteria Catholics in the United States have recognized the fact that our democracy has given us the advantage over the totalitarian situation that exists in Southeast Asia and other parts of the world. Priests, nuns, clerics, and laypeople of all ages have begun to join in protests against those who would put order above justice and righteousness. The trouble is not just with the world and the people in it but with some of the Church authorities. And the unfair tactic of those who would disrupt has always been to demand that those who describe virtue and righteousness live by those standards. I think we must all be humble enough to realize that all of us have to live by the same standards that we are preaching.

In other words, in the last analysis we must recognize the power and the influence of Jesus Christ as it is portrayed in the Gospel. Anyone seeking for truth, justice, and new hope for equality in the world cannot forget that it was our Lord who said, "The truth shall set us free." The urge to make the Church live up to the standards of its Lord always exists where the life of faith is lived out, even in our worst moments.

What I am pointing out is that by the time I was entering my third decade of ministry as a priest, I was in a church that allowed the priest who so chose to create a little holy disorder. While being too timid to openly challenge the structure on most issues, I was freed to attempt to implement the spirit of these new possibilities within the local situations in which I found myself. Surrounded by chaos in the secular world, I was not as bound to order in the ecclesiastical sphere as I once had been. Even without the support of immediate superiors, I had the precedent of the Church's voice to open some windows to see what a little light might produce.

I do not want people to model after me or duplicate what I have tried to do. That is too limiting, and I am not worthy of any kind of emulation. I do want people to catch the dream of something new and better, something that serves the Lord with more effectiveness and shows to a cynical world a Church more authentic. And, thankfully, day by day that dream is being realized. More and more as time goes by the church and its clergy *are* presenting the faith in a way that all can feel the *Love of God*.